WITHDRAWN

Rollo turned to look at the churning river,
with its cold layer of fog. He could swear there were
chunks of ice floating in the Rawchill River.

The dozen trolls stood in a circle, holding hands like children. Rollo could feel the strength of his fellow trolls, and he knew they were a noble race.

He wasn't sure how long they stood there, shivering in the darkness, but he felt a strange lightness in his stomach. He turned to look at the aged wizard. Stygius Rex's eyes rolled back in his head, and his mouth formed strange, guttural sounds. With a jerk, the sorcerer threw his arms skyward.

At that same moment, Rollo's feet lifted him off the ground. He gripped the hands of those around him, trying to pull all of them with him. "We can do it," he said aloud. "We trolls can do anything we want."

He was flying, and it was wonderful!

THE
TROLL KING
JOHN VORNHOLT

ALADDIN PAPERBACKS
New York London Toronto Sydney Singapore

This book is a work of fiction. Any references to historical events, real people, or real locales are used fictitiously. Other names, characters, places, and incidents are the product of the author's imagination, and any resemblance to actual events or locales or persons, living or dead, is entirely coincidental.

First Aladdin Paperbacks edition August 2002

Text copyright © 2002 by John Vornholt

ALADDIN PAPERBACKS
An imprint of Simon & Schuster
Children's Publishing Division
1230 Avenue of the Americas
New York, NY 10020

Printed in the United States of America
10 9 8 7 6 5 4 3 2 1

Library of Congress Control Number: 2002101646

ISBN 0-7434-2412-3

For Lisa

CHAPTER 1

THE KEEP OF STYGIUS REX

*T*HUD-SQUISH, *THUD-SQUISH* CAME THE HEAVY FOOTSTEPS OF the ogre as he marched down the dark, slimy tunnel. His hulking shape was outlined on the wall by the light from his torch, and he had to duck his bushy head to avoid the dripping moss on the ceiling.

The ogre's footsteps were followed by the scuffling noises of a little gnome named Runt, who struggled to keep up. His tiny oil lamp barely lit the greasy walls of the tunnel, which smelled like rancid boar snout mixed with wet dog. These were smells the gnome *usually* liked, but today the old scribe was in a bad mood. He hated it when the master sent for him in the middle of the day, when normal folks should be asleep!

Runt spotted a fat, black beetle skittering through the

scum on the floor. Swiftly he speared the bug with a curled claw and popped it into his mouth, crunching loudly. Burst it all, he didn't know *when* he would get breakfast!

"Why is the master awake at this hour?" grumbled the hunched little gnome. "If those crazy banshees were wailing, I'm going to send them into the Great Chasm!"

"You wouldn't do that," said the massive ogre, sounding horrified at the idea. "Not banshees—good dream."

"A good dream!" muttered Runt. "Good grief! Why in the underworld is he having *good dreams?* Doesn't he have spells to keep good things away?" Each time Runt said the word "good," his rubbery face scrunched into a scowl.

"I know nothing. What Stygius Rex sends me to get, I get." The big ogre grunted and took even longer strides, forcing Runt to run to keep up.

That's the way it is in the land of Bonespittle, thought the gnome. *Whatever Stygius Rex wants, Stygius Rex gets.* Everyone said he was a great sorcerer, but who knew for sure? For the last two hundred years, Stygius Rex had been the *only* sorcerer in Bonespittle.

A mysterious food poisoning had claimed the others at a banquet, leaving the sly young sorcerer in charge. Now Stygius Rex was old and lumpy with warts, and Runt suspected he was only a mediocre magic user. But Stygius made up for his faults with cunning and cruelty.

Even before they reached the quarters of the sorcerer, Runt smelled the distinct odor of a ghoul. They gave off a rotting stench, which made sense because ghouls were mostly dead. They smelled riper than rancid boar's snout, and the only way to stop a ghoul was to cut him up and scatter the pieces. Runt heard a door creak open, followed by dripping and gurgling sounds, and he knew it was the worst of the lot—General Drool.

The gnome's bulbous nose wrinkled, and his pointed ears curled downward. Even to a gnome who lived underground, General Drool was creepy.

Dashing after the big ogre, Runt rounded a corner and saw a hint of light ahead. The hairy ogre stopped and bowed to a cloaked figure who blocked the light from escaping the open door. The ogre pointed to Runt and backed away, still bowing.

The ominous figure turned with a creaking sound and looked down at Runt. The little gnome tried not to cringe, but it was hard to look at the ghoul's rotting face and rheumy yellow eyes. Plus, he had gotten his name for a good reason: Drool oozed from slack lips that barely covered his sharpened teeth.

Runt winced a little when a drop of Drool's drool plopped on his pointed slippers. The skeletal mouth seemed to smile at the insult, and the ghoul gurgled a whisper: "The master sent for only the two of us. What took you so long?"

"I was asleep," muttered Runt. "What should I be doing in the middle of the day?"

Thudding noises came from inside, making Runt jump with surprise. Then he realized it was the sorcerer's staff, pounding the earthen floor of his abode. "Get in here!" croaked his aged voice.

Runt's legs twitched, and he almost charged ahead of the ghoul. But he jumped back and let General Drool lead the way with his black cloak swirling behind him. Runt tried not to slip in the pool of spittle left behind.

The sorcerer's lair looked more like a laboratory than a bedroom. There were tables with beakers and vials suspended in metal stands; they contained squirming tentacles and inky liquids. Some vials were resting over small oil lamps, and they boiled and bubbled, shooting horrible fumes into the already foul air. Oddities hung from the ceiling, and the tall ghoul had to duck under a blown-up puffer fish and a shrunken head.

Cockeyed shelves lined the walls, and they were packed with colorful jars of herbs, roots, seeds, and pickled newts. Stretched across a hole in the rear wall was a red curtain, covered in ancient symbols and runes. Runt had no idea what any of the symbols meant, but he knew the curtain covered the entrance to Stygius Rex's inner lair, a place the gnome would never dare to go.

In a far corner of the room, the great sorcerer sat on a stool at his sloping table. He called it his plotting table. Flickering lamplight made his face look more sunken and cadaverous than usual, and bristling gray eyebrows cloaked his eyes. Hair sprouted in tufts from numerous moles on his lantern jaw, but his spotted skull was hairless. People often said that Stygius Rex had some troll in him—and he looked it—but they never said that to his face.

Maybe 150 years ago the young sorcerer had been somewhat handsome, but now he was old and blighted. Stygius Rex was the only one of his race left alive in Bonespittle, so he was an object of incredible awe and fear.

Runt gazed upward from the sorcerer's black riding boots, encrusted with silver runes, to his red silk pants and yellow tunic. His outfit was highlighted by a black cloak lined with blazing red silk. When he raised his head and jutted his wart-covered jaw, his red eyes burned with madness.

"Welcome," said Stygius Rex, sounding unusually cheerful. "You look well, General Drool. Fit as a pitfall. Hello, Runt, sorry to have woken you. Get out your book."

Runt often wondered why he wrote down any of this, because he and Stygius Rex were the only ones in the land who could read. If it was important, they would probably remember it. Nevertheless, the lumpen gnome got out his book, dipped his quill in a vial of ink, and wrote down the phase of the moon.

The sorcerer swept his hand grandly through the air. "Just before I went to bed, I cast a superb prophecy spell. I'm sure it was effective, because I never have cheery dreams like this. I dreamt that a mighty leader emerged from Bonespittle, and people all over the land were cheering him. I saw him crowned at his glorious inauguration . . . from a great distance, like a bird flying overhead."

5

The sorcerer quickly added, "Of course, I can fly . . . but not usually so high as in this vision. I followed a column of travelers, and I soared over the Great Chasm. Below me was a sparkling new bridge, uniting our land and theirs, and it was full of pilgrims going in each direction."

He speared a crooked finger triumphantly into the air. "At that instant, I knew what I had done to make myself so beloved. I, Stygius Rex, *built* that bridge across the Great Chasm!"

Runt chuckled under his breath. "You built a bridge over the Great Chasm? Surely, Master, this was a *symbolic* dream. You've had many prophetic dreams that . . . er, we have yet to interpret. Besides, you already *are* the ultimate despot of Bonespittle. Your subjects tremble at your name and live in absolute dread of you. What else could make you more kingly?"

The old sorcerer's burning eyes narrowed, and his hairy warts bristled. He leaned down from his stool and peered at Runt with sneering disdain. "They don't *love* me. I'm tired of seeing sniveling fear and knocking knees—why can't my subjects ever *smile* at me?

"Besides," he scoffed, straightening, "this prophecy was different. The spell worked, I could *feel* it! I saw people coming and going on that bridge—do you know what that means?"

Runt cowered, knowing he should keep his mouth shut. "That they have to pay a toll to cross?"

"That, too, but the important thing is that I will add the Bonny Woods, land of the fairy and elf, to *my* domain. My kingdom will double in size overnight!" Gleefully the sorcerer rubbed his hands together. At his side, General Drool smacked his rubbery lips at the thought.

"You're going to *attack* them?" asked Runt with a squeak of alarm. "Fairies and elves are ferocious fighters who will cut us up and feed us to their children! They have horrible magic and will turn us into toadstools and dung heaps!"

The sorcerer chuckled with delight, and the ghoul gave an amused wheeze. "You old fool!" said Stygius Rex. "Do you really believe the fairy tales we tell our children? The residents of the Bonny Woods have magic, yes, but they are not of *my* caliber. The elves are good archers, but . . . never mind that. At the moment, we intend to build a *friendly* bridge—to promote friendship."

Runt's bulbous face twisted into a grimace. "Ooh, that really was a *good* dream you had. I remember when you dreamt that you turned all the butterflies into bats!" He made a few notes. "I will make sure to write it down, Master, and we can archive this dream with the others."

"You weren't listening," said Stygius Rex with an icy edge to his voice. "I intend to *build* that bridge across the Great Chasm. We will crawl out of this hole in the ground to visit my loyal subjects—to enlist their support. Bring the entire keep hold, because we will be above ground for how ever long it takes to build that bridge."

The gnome gulped, thinking that this was really bad. The sorcerer was serious. "And if this adventure ends up in war with the fairies and elves, are you ready for that?"

"Who said anything about *war?*" asked the sorcerer magnanimously. "I saw no fighting in this dream, and there are other ways to subdue your enemies. Aren't there, General Drool?"

The ghoul gurgled a reply: "I can think of several."

The sorcerer's red eyes gazed far away, as he seemed to see beyond the earthen walls. "Perhaps this bridge will answer the mystery of the Great Chasm. Our oldest tales say that Bonespittle and the Bonny Woods were once joined, and there was no gorge between them. Who, or what, cleaved that great barrier?"

Runt twittered nervously. "These mysteries are not to be known, Your Wickedness!"

"No matter. I will still be the one who joins both lands into a new kingdom—*mine!*" Stygius Rex turned to his ghoulish general and wagged a finger. "Drool, you go saddle Old Belch."

For a moment, the ghoul actually blanched a shade to pure white. "Old Belch?" he asked with a shudder.

"Yes, now hurry!" roared the great sorcerer, rising to his feet. He straightened his cloak and waved his arms regally over Runt's head. "My subjects await. And so does my destiny!"

CHAPTER 2
TROLL TOWN

F OLKS HAVE ALWAYS WONDERED WHY TROLLS LIVE UNDER
bridges. In Dismal Swamp there wasn't anywhere else to
live. The whole village was nothing but a web of wood-and-
vine suspension bridges, stretching from one spit of land to
another. The land itself was mostly the rotting ruins of old
bridges that had fallen down long ago. Now they were
entwined with mud, vines, and tree roots to make these pathetic
humps of land.

The proper denizens of Bonespittle—ogres, gnomes, and
ghouls—lived underground and only went out at night. Trolls
had a hard time maintaining such normal habits. They often
had to work days, doing labor nobody else would do. As best
they could, they carved out hovels in the mounds between the
bridges, where it was always cold and damp.

Plus, the murky water of the swamp lay at their doorsteps. The mire wasn't deep—except in a few places—but the snappers and suckers didn't need much space.

A young troll named Rollo shivered with fear as he thought about the dangers lurking beneath and above him. Although he pretended to be asleep, his mind raced with images of things he could do now that it was daylight. He could smell flowers, chase the dragonflies, or take a nap where it was warm and dry!

The troll squirmed in his sleeping pit, because he was getting very large for his age—fourteen years. He would have to find a new crevice soon, or get out of here altogether. It would shock his parents, but maybe he would volunteer to work days, above ground. That had to be less boring than his apprenticeship as a bridge builder.

"All these stupid rules are annoying," grumbled the youth. "Maybe I should just go up and sleep on the bridge today, despite them."

Then he cringed with alarm. "But what if I meet an angry billy goat?"

In truth, Rollo was mainly scared of the ogre patrols, but he thought he could avoid them. If the ogres caught you running about in broad daylight, you'd better have a good reason. Some trolls worked days, but they were always guarded by ogres or ghouls. Yes, going above ground at noon by oneself was a foolish thing to do.

Why do the ghouls and ogres treat us so badly? wondered

Rollo. *True, trolls aren't as frightful as ogres or as hideous as ghouls, but we're plenty ugly. We're hairy, big-nosed, potbellied, and skinny-legged! What else do they want?*

Actually Rollo was not as hairy, big-nosed, potbellied, and skinny-legged as most trolls. He was big all over, and plain-looking. Unlike most trolls, who had large forearms and skinny biceps, Rollo's arms were like tree trunks. Someone who wasn't a troll might consider him the handsomest of the lot.

Driven by his anger, Rollo crawled out of his sleeping pit, being careful not to scrape his talons on the straw mats. Although the entrance to the cave was shut tightly, a bit of daylight seeped through the slats in the wood. He could make out their humble living quarters, carved from a soggy mound of debris. It smelled like mold, wet fur, and snail grease.

There was a fire pit in the center of the room, where a few embers still glowed. Vines and tree roots poked through the earthen walls. From the vines hung clothes, cooking utensils, and a huge portrait of Stygius Rex. That was the biggest thing in the house.

He stopped at the grub bucket to see if there were any succulent vermin left from dinner. But they had eaten them all. There were never enough grubs, it seemed.

Rollo could hear the snoring of his parents and older sister, Crawfleece. They were curled up in their sleeping pits—just hairy mounds in the darkness. Quietly, he pulled on his pants and tiptoed toward the slivers of light.

This was the hardest part, opening the old door without alerting anyone. But Rollo had thought of this and put snail grease on the hinges and bolt. The bolt opened as smoothly as leech pie slipping down the throat. The hinges squeaked just a little.

Now he had to block the sunlight when he opened the door. Luckily, the young troll was big enough to block a lot of sunlight. With his arm above his head, Rollo contorted himself into a crescent shape in order to slip out the door.

The big troll carefully pulled the door shut behind him and breathed the warm, sunny air. He inhaled some rank swamp gas, too, which burned his nose hairs, but Rollo shook it off. He squinted into the blazing sun and bright blue sky, and thought, *Ah, it's good to be awake at noon!*

Dazzled by the sun, the young troll slipped backward and almost rolled down the muddy bank. At the last second his hands caught a vine, and only his feet hit the brackish water. He pulled them out with a sucking sound. The water was as thick and dark as bark syrup, except where it was covered with green slime.

Something roiled under the surface, and the tip of a scale swished past. At once Rollo scrambled to his feet and dashed up steps worn into the tree roots. The tree at the top was little more than a withered stump, but it must have been huge once.

The higher Rollo climbed, the warmer the sun felt on his hairy back. Some insects buzzed around his head, but he swatted them off. He finally reached the poles that supported the south bridge, but he didn't jump to his feet. Instead, he peered cautiously over the top of the tree stump.

Stretching in every direction were low-slung wooden bridges, supported only by the next mound. Gnarled trees, small wagons, and empty vegetable stands were scattered across this lumpy landscape. In the distance were the fog-covered treetops of Forgotten Forest, and to the east were the snowcapped peaks of the Sore Knuckle Mountains.

This strange network of wood and vines was Troll Town, the only place Rollo had ever lived. It looked so peaceful now, with no one in sight and the sun beating down. Almost magical.

The trolls were poor, but they worked hard to maintain their bridges. That was important, because there was nothing below the swaying vines but the quagmire and its stench. Most trolls who fell into the morass lived to tell about it, but some were sucked under without a trace. The thick water bubbled ominously.

Rollo was cautious as he pulled himself up the vines and onto the southern bridge. Which way should he go? His family's hillock supported three bridges dipping toward the northwest, south, and northeast. If he wanted to go some other direction, he first had to go to someone else's mound.

Because he was already on the southern bridge, Rollo went that direction. He tiptoed very quietly on the swaying slats, because some trolls were light sleepers—hence, the reputation of trolls for bothering strangers who crossed their bridges. They really weren't out to harm anyone, just to complain about being awakened.

His next footstep brought a creak from the old wood, and Rollo nearly jumped out of his fur. He gripped the vine handholds and whirled in every direction, but he could see no one in the quiet village. The young troll breathed a sigh of relief and continued on his way.

"I'm down here, stupid!" called a voice, causing Rollo to gasp. That voice had come from below him!

His knobby knees shaking, the big troll leaned over the bridge to look down. Standing at the door of his hovel was his big sister, Crawfleece, shaking a hairy fist at him. She was a very popular teenage troll—big-nosed, big-boned, skinny-legged, with a rotten disposition.

"Why are you sneaking around in the middle of the day?" she demanded with a sisterly sneer.

"I, uh—" Rollo gulped, because he couldn't tell her the truth. In order to keep Crawfleece from turning him in, he had to say something she would like. To buy time, he said, "Quiet, you'll wake up Mom and Dad."

She made sure the door was shut, then turned back to him. "You're in trouble."

"No, no . . . I was going to . . . to skim the Hole!"

Crawfleece laughed out loud. "Oh, I was afraid you were going to smell flowers again. Why didn't you say you wanted to skim the Hole? I'll go with you!" In a blink, she climbed up the vines and joined him on the bridge.

Rollo suppressed a groan, because now he had to go to the Hole and prove his bravery. He really wanted to smell flowers and chase dragonflies, not risk his life. But Crawfleece was already skipping along the bridge, caring little who heard or saw them.

"Come on!" she called, waving to him to follow.

Rollo's big shoulders slumped as he traipsed after his sister. What had started out as a private little adventure was now turning into his sister's outing. Didn't it always happen that way? Of course, he didn't have to tell her he was skimming the Hole. He should have said *anything* but that.

Swinging merrily on the suspension bridges, Crawfleece led her brother across the sleeping village. At least she knew the fastest shortcuts, and they were gone by the time the drowsy trolls rolled out of their pits and tried to catch them.

Still, Rollo's dread mounted as they left the bridge and entered a fog-shrouded woods. Forgotten Forest was the most dismal part of Dismal Swamp, which made it the most dismal part of all of Bonespittle. It was a depressing collection of quicksand pools, mangy trees covered with moss, and thick mist that smelled like rotten eggs. And bugs, lots of bugs.

There wasn't much sunlight in Forgotten Forest, no matter what time of day it was. There was a trail, however, and Rollo was careful to stick to it. He could hear the quicksand bubbling and slurping just under the dead leaves at the side of the trail.

He usually avoided this place, although there were some lovely wildflowers growing along the trail. For some reason, it drizzled all the time in Forgotten Forest. Maybe it was moisture from the steamy swamp condensing on the leaves. The trees were tall and skinny, and hanging vines slapped Rollo in the face as he walked.

Something rustled in the weeds, and a few frogs hopped by. Crawfleece deftly kicked her foot and speared one with a long talon. She popped it into her mouth, crunched a few times, and had breakfast without slowing down. Rollo wasn't even hungry.

"What's wrong with you, Brother?" asked Crawfleece, picking her teeth with a purple claw. "You never seem to be happy anymore."

The teenage troll shrugged his beefy shoulders, while a mossy branch slapped him in the face. "Who wouldn't be happy with a life like this? I can grow up to make bridges, just like everybody else in the family. I can go anywhere I want, as long as I sneak around in the daytime. I can associate with ogres—as long as they're my boss."

"Hey," growled Crawfleece, "we're very lucky to all work on the bridges. Would you like to tend crops or wait on ogres? They don't tip very well, I can tell you."

"Okay, okay," muttered Rollo. "You know everything, even though you haven't seen any more of Bonespittle than I have."

She whirled on him and tried to shove him off the path, but Rollo caught her arm and deflected it with lightning speed. The big troll scoffed at her. "Sis, it's been a long time since you could do that. Don't try it again."

Crawfleece snarled, showing enormous square teeth. She was troubled at the ease with which he had evaded her, he could tell. There was one good thing about growing up: no more being pushed into the quicksand!

In due time, they came to their destination. The Hole was just that: a large excavation in the ground about fifty feet across. Some gnome engineer had thought it would drain off a lot of swamp water and create more land. It had only half worked, and now the Hole was partially filled with the vilest water and the meanest monsters in all of Bonespittle.

Tall trees grew around the Hole, and some branches stretched over it. It was possible, although not smart, to grab a vine and swing out over the Hole, skimming it with the rear end. Assorted slimy beasts tried to get you, but they were a split-second slow . . . usually.

From the sound of giggles, Rollo could tell they weren't the only ones who thought skimming the Hole was more fun than sleeping. His knees buckled when they reached the bank, and he saw who was there. It was Ludicra and three of her friends.

Ludicra was only the most spectacularly ugly troll in all of Bonespittle. She had ears like a donkey, fur like a yak, and incredibly beady eyes. This princess was exactly Rollo's age, and he had a fearsome crush on her. In fact, she was the only girl he ever thought about, although he had said fewer than a dozen words to her.

Crawfleece pinched Rollo and whispered, "Ah, now I see why you wanted to come here." She took off, tugging on vines as she ran, testing them for strength. "I'm going first!"

Ludicra and her friends giggled, and Rollo was sure his skin was turning six shades of purple. Nevertheless, he strode bravely forward and said cordially. "Hello, Ludicra. And . . . and Histeria, Nostris, and Mealyworm."

The lovely Ludicra smiled snidely. "I didn't know you went in for this kind of thing. Uh, what's your name?"

Pained, he still managed to blurt out, "Rollo. We've been apprentices together for two years."

"Oh, who pays any attention to *that?*" she said with a sniff. Her friends twittered with approval. "So are you going to go? We'll watch you."

"He's not brave enough," said Nostris, obviously staring deep into his soul.

Rollo gulped, faced with this dreadful decision and no way to escape. The only other time he had skimmed the Hole he'd been terrified, and he had been a lot smaller then. With a twitch, he gazed into the opaque depths of the water, which teemed with unseen but terrifying life.

"I'm going now!" screamed his sister. "Watch me!"

Rollo breathed a sigh of relief, having been reprieved for at least a few seconds. His big sister had selected a stout vine clinging to a branch that extended over the Hole. As soon as she saw she had their attention, she grabbed the vine and jumped off the steep bank.

With a yell, Crawfleece soared over the brackish pond. At the last second she lifted her legs and dropped her rear until she whooshed across the water, sending up plumes. A monstrous alligator snapped at her, and a tentacle lashed at her, which brought gales of laughter from Crawfleece.

As she flew off the vine onto the other bank, she shouted, "Catch the vine!"

Rollo's feet refused to move. In fact, one of them tried to go the other way, and he almost fell down. Lunging forward, Ludicra managed to grab the vine as it soared past.

"Here," said Ludicra with a gleam in her eye. "I'm sure you meant to catch this." Her friends giggled with satisfaction as she handed the vine to Rollo.

"Yeah, fine," he muttered. "I'm getting too big for this, you know. We're all getting too big."

"Come on, you lizard gizzard! Go!" screamed his dear sister from the opposite bank.

He couldn't refuse. In their small village, such an act of cowardice would be known by everyone before the sun went down. Trolls weren't supposed to be smart, just eager to prove themselves. Rollo screwed up his courage and tugged convincingly on the vine a few times. He didn't know what that proved, but it made him feel better.

It's all over in a second, he told himself. *Don't bother to skim—just keep yourself out of the water.*

Rollo gripped the vine as high as he could, glad that his fingers were strong. He also planned to grip with his legs for as long as he could, without getting wet. *I'm going to soar over that water!*

When Rollo heard Ludicra and her friends start to whisper, he knew his time was running out. With a frightened squeal, the big troll flung himself over the edge of the bank.

At first, he did soar, and it was fun—until he opened his eyes. Zooming into view was an alligator with a head like an old bellows. The beast was thrashing about as if it couldn't believe its luck. Rollo panicked, and he tried to climb the vine instead of just hang on. That caused him to slip at the same moment he forgot to lift his feet.

Instead of skimming the water, he splashed into it up to his waist. His momentum carried him for a few feet until a pair of mighty jaws crunched down on his pants and a tentacle wrapped around his neck.

With a gurgle and a helpless wave, Rollo let go of the vine and vanished under the swirling black water.

CHAPTER 3
PAST GLORIES

I'M GOING TO DROWN, THE YOUNG TROLL DECIDED AS A SNAP-per and a sucker struggled to keep him under the murky water. Rollo's fourteen years of mundane life passed before his eyes. To no surprise, it was mainly devoted to digging for grubs. Plus there were endless hours spent repairing bridges.

What a pitiful life it is, thought Rollo glumly. *And now I'm about to die in front of my beloved Ludicra.* The embarrassment was almost worse than the slimy tentacles around his neck and the sharp teeth in his pelt.

Fortunately, Rollo had taken a big breath when he leaped off the bank. Somehow he suspected he would land in the water, so he'd been mentally prepared. Although he had panicked when clinging to the vine, the troll was surprisingly calm as two swamp monsters tried to end his young life.

Twisting underwater, he got his hands on the gator's jaws and yanked the teeth off his rear. That was painful, because a big chunk of fur went it. Enraged, the troll hoisted the creature out of the water and hurled him toward the bank. The gator sailed clear out of the Hole and crashed against a tree.

Rollo used that chance to break the surface and grab a breath of air. A second later, the sucker tightened its grip on his neck and tried to drag him deeper into the vile waters.

Feeling himself being dragged under, the troll struggled with all his might. Although Rollo's feet could not touch bottom, he kicked hard enough to break the surface once more. Stroking his thick arms, he shot from the water like a flying fish. Still, a big, tentacled sucker fish clung to his back and neck.

With brute strength, Rollo managed to swim a bit while the creature tried to drag him down. He heard a shriek and looked up to see Crawfleece come soaring across the Hole, swinging on a vine. She reached down and snatched the beast as she flew past, and Rollo was lifted out of the water by the slimy tentacle around his neck.

The monster hated being out of its element, and it thrashed wildly, slapping the troll in the face. Finally the sucker let go, and Rollo was dumped back into the water. Crawfleece, though, hung on to her prize.

Fortunately, Rollo was close enough to the bank to grab some vines and haul himself out. He heard Ludicra and her friends chortling with delight at this rich entertainment.

Sweating, panting, half-drowned, Rollo crawled out of the swamp and collapsed on the muddy bank.

From the corner of his eye, he saw Crawfleece beating something against a tree trunk. "Thanks to you, little brother, we'll have sucker fish for breakfast!"

Rollo heard giggles, and he rolled over to see Ludicra staring down at him. Her friends hovered in the background, their pointed ears twitching attentively. "Are you all right?" asked Ludicra with a delighted grin.

"Y-Yes," he gurgled, spitting out a mouthful of putrid water. "I think so."

Suddenly a stricken look came over Ludicra's face, and she dashed away from the young troll. Her friends shrieked, and all of them bolted into the trees at once.

"Ludicra!" he called helplessly, but she was gone. Rollo looked around in confusion, trying to find his sister, but Crawfleece had also disappeared. When he heard crashing sounds in the bushes, along with guttural voices, he knew why they had run.

Ogres!

Still covered in swamp water, Rollo rolled over and staggered to his feet. He immediately slipped in the mud and landed face-first on the ground. As the voices grew louder, the young troll could barely stand up. He took one step when a loud voice shouted, "Halt!"

He whirled around and saw four giant ogres in black uniforms come crashing through the forest. They were so fat that their studded uniforms hugged the flab around their middles. Their big tusks curled upward toward pug noses, which wrinkled with distaste at the sight of the young troll.

One of them pointed a crossbow at Rollo and fired what looked like a bundle of rags. The bundle exploded in midair and turned into a net, which wrapped around Rollo's broad shoulders and ensnared his legs. He shuffled a few inches, but could barely move his feet. With a crash, the big troll fell back to the ground.

Laughing heartily, the ogres strode up to the helpless troll and prodded him with their hobnailed boots. He glared at them. "I wasn't running away. You . . . you didn't need to do that."

"And what were you doing out here?" growled the biggest of the ogres.

Rollo gulped, unsure what he should say. The suspicious ogres began to look around, and one of them walked toward a big tree at the edge of the Hole. Rollo could see him prodding something on the ground, but he couldn't get a good look because of the net wrapped around him.

"I can tell you what this troll was doing," said the ogre by the tree. "He was poaching the master's alligators! He was planning to have alligator stew for breakfast."

Triumphantly, the ogre lifted the tail of the alligator, which Rollo had hurled against the tree. It was either dead or dazed.

"No, no!" protested the youth. "We were . . . I mean *I* was skimming across the pond on a vine, and I fell in. That beast tried to eat me!"

"You see there, he was trying to *poison* the alligator!" said another ogre, and they all laughed.

In desperation, Rollo began to struggle in the net, trying to crawl away from the patrol. The head ogre reached down and gave the net a yank, which pulled Rollo's arms out from under him. Once again, he flopped face-first into the mud.

"What are we going to do with this poacher?" asked the head ogre, his quills bristling. "Should we make him work in the lye factory or the brimstone pits?"

"If he likes animals so much, maybe he should take care of the sorcerer's dragons," said another. Rollo shivered, although he had never actually seen a dragon.

"Yes, he could give them baths and trim their talons," suggested a third. "And put out their flames at daylight."

"What about digging latrines?" asked the fourth ogre. "He looks strong enough to do some honest work."

"I'm too young to work!" protested Rollo. "I'm only fourteen."

That brought a scowl to the leader's rumpled face, and his tusks clinked against his fangs. "You're not too young to be running around in broad daylight, are you? You steal alligator meat from our noble master, Stygius Rex, but you won't *work* for him? We should throw you back into the Hole, tied up as you are."

Rollo remembered that ogres loved all kinds of contests, especially games of strength. He blurted, "If I beat you in arm wrestling, will you let me go?"

A look of shock passed over the ogre's beefy face and bloodshot eyes. Rollo flinched, certain he would be tossed back into the Hole immediately. Instead, the ogre scratched his stubbled topknot of quills and broke into a grin. "Get this! An ugly little troll—still wet behind the ears—thinks he can best the captain of the guard in arm wrestling?"

His fellows laughed heartily along with their boss. Two of them picked Rollo up and yanked off his net, whirling him around in the process. The young troll nearly fell back into the Hole, but he staggered to his feet and focused his eyes. The big captain marched slowly toward him.

It's one thing to arm wrestle the other apprentices, thought Rollo, *but this is a grizzled ogre who outweighs me by a ton. He'll probably tear my arm off!*

Rollo took a deep breath, reminding himself that he had mastered the art of arm wrestling. It was all in the wrist. Once he forced an opponent's hand back, the arm would follow. Trolls had powerful forearms, and Rollo had a beefy upper arm to go along with his.

As he rose to his full height, the troll was glad to see he was a bit taller than the ogre, although the brute was still a lot wider. Seen at close range, the ogre's curled tusks were kind of interesting; they were chipped and yellowing, covered with brown slime.

The ogre blinked at Rollo with wide, bloodshot eyes. "You get your freedom if you beat me. Tee-hee! So what do I get when I beat *you?*"

"Ah . . . ah," stammered the troll. "You get the . . . alligator!"

An alligator was moving toward them at that precise moment. The big snapper lashed around like a whip, and chomped the hindquarters of the nearest ogre, who howled like a banshee and threw his crossbow into the air. It hit a branch, shot off, and a net came swirling down over two more ogres.

The captain rushed to the aid of his comrades and was soon rolling around in the mud, wrestling the angry reptile. While they were occupied, Rollo did the only sensible thing: He ran off through the woods.

But the troll only got a few steps before he was seized with guilt over the ruckus he had caused. What if they needed help? Rollo crouched down and doubled back, being certain to keep out of sight in the bramble bushes. Since he was already covered with muck, he blended well into the thick undergrowth.

He heard loud grunts, and he saw two ogres toss the alligator back into the Hole. Still snapping its jaws, the beast writhed in midair before splashing into the black water and disappearing. A third ogre was trying to patch their wounded comrade, who would not be sitting down for a while.

"Where did he go?" growled the captain, searching the forest with rage. "Where is that worthless poacher?"

Rollo hunkered down in the bushes, trying to become invisible.

"Oh, he ran off as soon as the snapper came to life," answered another. "He's probably halfway to Troll Town by now."

"Pity him if we ever meet again," said the captain of the guard with a snarl. Rollo was suddenly very glad that he hadn't arm wrestled the brute. "Back to camp," he ordered.

"I can't walk!" howled the ogre with the alligator teeth marks in his backside.

"Then stay here and rot," growled the captain. Gracefully—for a fat ogre—he swiveled on his heel and stomped off into the forest. The patrol followed him, including the wounded one, who whimpered and whined as he shuffled along.

Making his way cautiously, Rollo didn't reach home until mid-afternoon. Predictably, his father, mother, and sister were all waiting for him in their tiny hovel at the base of the bridge. Obviously, Crawfleece had spread the news about his little adventure, but she probably had left out the part where she had encouraged him to skim the Hole.

"You're by yourself?" asked his father, Nulneck, with surprise. He quickly shut the door behind the young troll and locked it. His father was somewhat shriveled and bookish for a troll. He would never be called an engineer, but he often helped design new bridges when repairs weren't good enough. Rollo had always considered his father to be wiser than most trolls.

Rollo had gotten his size from his mother, Vulgalia, who

was a head taller than his father and even broader than his sister. She continued to glower at him, waiting for an answer.

"Yes, I'm alone," he answered sheepishly.

"Where have you been?" demanded Crawfleece, with a wounded air only an older sister can muster. "Didn't the ogres catch you?"

"Yes, they caught me," said Rollo. "No thanks to *you!* Instead of running off, you could have done something—"

"Don't blame her!" snapped his mother. "How did you get away from them?"

"An alligator attacked them, and they forgot about me for a moment."

"Clever lad," said his father, putting his arm around Rollo's shoulders. "We're glad you're all right, but you took an awful risk. It wouldn't be good for this family if you were arrested by a patrol. Not good at all. You could lose your apprenticeship . . . I could lose my job. Understand?"

Contritely, Rollo nodded. Then he sniffed the stale air in the tight quarters and thought he smelled something fishy. His mother broke down and gave him a smile. "If nobody's with you, let's cook that sucker fish!" said Vulgalia with a wink.

"I'll get the water!" chirped Crawfleece, scuttling outside with a bucket.

"I'll light the fire!" said Nulneck cheerfully.

As Rollo and his family finished eating the slimy delicacy, they told stories about past encounters with ogres. In every story, the ogres were persecuting poor trolls. The more Rollo heard, the angrier he got.

"Why are they always our bosses?" he demanded. "Who put *them* in charge?" He glanced back nervously at the portrait of Stygius Rex hanging on a vine poking through the wall. "I can see the sorcerer being important, but trolls are as good as ogres and ghouls."

"Keep your voice down," hissed Crawfleece, who became a model of virtue whenever Rollo got in trouble.

"It wasn't always that way," said his father thoughtfully. "Many years ago, trolls had their own king and were great warriors. They were respected and feared all over Bonespittle. Some say that trolls even had *magic.*"

"Nonsense," sniffed his mother. "If you want to believe those fairy tales, that's your business. But don't fill the children's heads with such silliness." His mother popped a fat tentacle into her mouth and slurped it down noisily.

"What happened to those magical trolls?" asked Rollo, entranced by this story.

Nulneck shrugged. "What always happens? The sorcerers banded together to conquer all of Bonespittle. They promised the ogres they would not be on the bottom of the pecking order if they helped the sorcerers. So they defeated the trolls and enslaved us, making us leave Fungus Meadows for this lousy swamp."

His mother snorted a laugh. "What a story. Imagine *us* living in Fungus Meadows! Do you notice, children, that your father does not offer one bit of proof to back up this fine retelling of history?"

Nulneck pointed at the stern portrait of Stygius Rex. "You only have to look at him to see that he's a troll."

"Ssshh!" she hissed. "The sorcerer has magical powers . . . maybe he can hear you! That is a very dangerous thing to say out loud."

"I still say that trolls were not always so downtrodden," insisted Nulneck. "If we had our own king, we'd have plenty of grubs and worms to eat!"

Rollo and Crawfleece exchanged amused looks at this bickering. Maybe it was the forbidden discussion, the dangerous lark in the forest, or the rich food that made them so happy. Whatever it was, they were having a fantastic meal that was a lot more fun than usual.

"I just don't like too much excitement," said his mother worriedly. "Although this sucker fish tastes really sweet." She chomped happily.

Everyone laughed, and Rollo breathed a sigh of relief, thankful that he hadn't gotten his family into trouble. "From now on, Mother," he promised her, "no more excitement. I'll do my apprenticeship and live a boring life. My days of adventure are over."

"That's a good boy," said Vulgalia, patting the troll on his knobby head.

CHAPTER 4

OLD BELCH

Even though he hardly slept that day, Rollo was ready to go out again when the sun went down. The only place he had to go was his apprentice job on the bridges, but even that would be fun. For one thing, Ludicra couldn't ignore him, because she had spoken to him only a few hours ago. She would have to marvel at his wondrous escape from the ogres.

Rollo packed a leftover tentacle in his lunch bag and kissed his mother good-bye. He whistled as he strolled along the bridges of Troll Town, saying hello to everyone he met. Other trolls seemed surprised to see anyone this cheerful first thing in the evening. They scowled and snorted at him in return.

As darkness fell over Dismal Swamp, the fire-keepers

lit the oil lamps. With stars sparkling overhead and the murky water hidden in shadows, the village began to look different, almost pretty. Every ugly mound became an oasis of light and glittering swarms of fireflies. Food stands along the bridges began to open, and the smell of roasted grubs wafted through the air.

Normally, Rollo drooled with hunger as he passed the food stands, but tonight his stomach was already full. And he had more delicious food in his pack. He was still excited from his adventures of the day, but he was ready to settle down and be a hardworking troll.

Soon he was in a shabby part of the village on the northern outskirts. Here the bridges were mostly old and run-down, and there weren't any food vendors. Few trolls lived here, so it was a good place for the apprentices to learn their craft. If they messed up a bridge out here, nobody important would fall into the swamp.

As he neared the work site, Rollo fluffed his bushy eyebrows and his ear hairs. The youngster wanted to look his best for Ludicra, and he knew he wasn't as hairy as most trolls. Maybe he would embellish his tale, telling her that he had fought off the ogres with his bare hands. Who would know?

The first person he saw was the master bridge builder, Krunkle. He was an old troll with a stooped brow, and tufts of white hair on his knobby head. He talked as if he had mud in his throat. Krunkle's philosophy was to work the apprentices hard so they would have to learn something.

"Rollo," growled Krunkle, "you're early tonight. Feel like working?"

"As a matter of fact, I do," answered Rollo. He looked around and could only see three other apprentices, none of whom were Ludicra.

"Start lashing planks." The old troll pointed to a pile of wood and a coil of rope. "If you need any drilled, give them to Mullmu."

Drilling sounded like more fun than lashing, but Rollo didn't complain. It was too beautiful a night, with the stars shining overhead and the fireflies dancing in the darkness. "Right, Master!" he said with a salute.

The old troll squinted at him. "Who put the squirm in your worm?"

Rollo grinned. "I didn't have to eat worms tonight. I had—"

Before he could finish, there was a shriek and several shouts to the north. Rollo and Krunkle whirled around to see a dozen trolls charging across the bridge, headed straight toward them. The old planks creaked ominously under the stampede, and the two trolls had to jump out of their way.

"What has gotten into you fools?" demanded Krunkle as they rushed past.

"He comes! He comes!" cried one blubbering troll who was covered in bark syrup. He must have been a farmer in Forgotten Forest, harvesting the syrup.

"Who comes?" asked Krunkle, stopping another frightened soul.

"Th-th-the sorcerer . . . Stygius Rex!" she shrieked.

The old troll turned a paler shade of gray, and his bushy eyebrows rolled up into the folds of his forehead.

Rollo scoffed in disbelief. "*Here?* The sorcerer is coming to Dismal Swamp?"

"Let me go!" yelled the frightened troll. "He'll turn us all into toadstools and dung heaps!" She pulled away from Krunkle's grasp and rejoined the mad stampede.

Rollo snorted a laugh. "Everyone knows it's *fairies* who turn you into toadstools and dung heaps. If Stygius Rex is coming here, he must just be passing through to . . . somewhere else."

"There's nowhere else," muttered Krunkle. "This is the big toe of Bonespittle. He wouldn't be coming here unless he had a reason. And if he's coming in this direction, he's going to cross over *this* bridge."

The old builder was suddenly a bundle of energy as he dashed to and fro. "Mullmu, shore up that center span! Rollo, stiffen those trusses! Filbum, patch that safety rail! Hegrok, check for rotten planks! Ludicra, you check all the stay ropes!"

Ludicra! Is she here? Rollo whirled in every direction, searching for his beloved. He finally spotted her at the rear mound, taking off her backpack. She flashed him a brief smile before picking up a coil of rope, and the young troll's heart soared higher than the stars.

"Rollo, the trusses!" snapped Krunkle, pounding him on his beefy shoulder.

"Yes, Master!" There was no reason not to start at Ludicra's end, was there? He grabbed a handful of tools and hustled to the opposite end of the bridge, where the plump troll was getting ready for work.

"What's the big emergency?" she whispered as she strapped on her tool belt.

"Some crazy farmers said that Stygius Rex is headed this way," answered Rollo breathlessly.

Her wonderfully ugly face twisted into a frown. "Right. And I'm the queen of Fungus Meadows. Did you get in trouble last day? I sure did."

All the fantastic tales Rollo planned to tell were suddenly forgotten in his concern for Ludicra. "No, I . . . I got away from them. What happened to you?"

"My parents caught me. I told them about you falling into the Hole, and the ogres catching you, so it didn't seem so bad. But I'm forbidden to ever see you again."

"Oh," muttered Rollo sadly. "But we never really talked before—"

Ludicra shrugged. "So it won't be a big change in our lives."

"Rollo! Get busy on those trusses!" bellowed Krunkle.

"Yes . . . yes, Master," he said absently as he picked up his tools and some wooden slats. In a fog of misery, the young troll went back to work.

Rollo had no idea how long he toiled on the old bridge before he again heard shouts and people running. When he looked up, he saw a parade on the dark horizon. At least it looked like a parade, or maybe a whole city on the move.

He could make out dozens of bright lamps carried high on poles, red and black banners fluttering in the breeze, plus a line of wagons and riders that stretched into the distance. In the middle of it all there appeared to be a huge float bobbing up and down.

To their credit, the marchers didn't charge willy-nilly over the shaky bridges of Troll Town. They marched slowly, spread out over several bridges. This made the procession look all the more impressive and regal, if somewhat lumbering.

A few brave trolls were beginning to gather from the south, drawn to the glittering parade. They wandered past the workers as if in a trance, anxious to see more, yet frightened at the same time. Rollo knew how they felt.

Their master, Krunkle, began to run around like a lunatic, throwing ropes and planks into the swamp. "Everyone, get out of here!" he ordered. "I don't want anyone around when these bridges collapse!"

To Rollo, that was the signal that he had the rest of the night off. He looked for Ludicra, but she had fled in the opposite direction—away from the sorcerer. The young troll joined the frightened mob that was shuffling forward to meet the master of Bonespittle.

"Is it really *him?*" they asked in hushed tones. "Why is he coming here?" everyone demanded at once.

"Who knows," muttered an old troll. "He can't banish us to anyplace worse than this swamp."

As Rollo crept forward with the others, he felt a tug on his arm. He turned to see his sister, Crawfleece. Of course, she would be brave enough to confront the sorcerer.

"Hey, brother," she said. "Did you get off work too?"

He nodded. "Great, huh?" But he still wasn't feeling great, not with Ludicra forbidden to talk to him.

Without warning, the night erupted with the loudest, most raucous belch anyone had ever heard. This enormous burp vibrated the hairs on Rollo's neck and caused his eyelids to fuse together. The monstrous noise was accompanied by a foul smell that blasted across the swamp, wiping out the worst swamp smells.

"Ewww!" groaned the crowd in unison. "What is *that?*"

Some of the trolls grinned, obviously enjoying the awful odor. But most of them turned and tried to run in the other direction. Luckily, Rollo was tall for a troll, and he was also close to one of the mounds. He grabbed his sister and hauled her to higher ground. They struggled to keep their footing as the mob surged past them.

Standing on his tiptoes, Rollo could see ghouls on horseback riding ahead of the procession. The clomping of hooves on the creaking bridges only made people more frightened. *But it wasn't a ghoul that made that giant belch,* thought Rollo.

He kept looking until he saw the source: a dark, squat shape silhouetted in the swaying lamplight. A slim figure sat astride the beast, which only made it look bigger. Others gathered around the monster, trying to push it, but it wasn't moving.

"What is it?" demanded Crawfleece.

"It looks like . . . a giant toad." Rollo squinted into the distance, trying to think what else it could be. "It's about fifteen feet across and eight feet tall. Built like a dung heap. They're trying to get it moving, but it won't budge."

"Smart toad," said Crawfleece. "These bridges aren't built for creatures that size. Uh, tell me, do you think it eats trolls?"

"I think it eats whatever it wants," answered Rollo.

Suddenly the lead ghoul was upon them, riding a prancing black horse that snorted smoke. He had a cadaverous face that was rotted away, and his yellow eyeballs glowed in their sockets. It was hard to believe that trolls were at the bottom of the social ladder when there were ghouls around. But this one was dressed in a long cape and a flashy, gold-trimmed uniform.

As he spoke, he sprayed drool in Rollo's face. "You trolls in front, move closer to the master! The rest of you—summon everyone in the village. Every troll alive must hear the words of Stygius Rex!"

The ghoul uncurled a long whip and snarled, "Move quickly!"

That was enough encouragement for Rollo to get moving. He wanted a closer look at the giant toad, anyway. Grabbing his sister's hand, he squeezed past the horse and ran down the bridge. After the whip cracked a few times, more trolls timidly followed them.

It took the better part of the night to gather together all the frightened trolls in the village and herd all of them around the visitors. Rollo spotted the ogres he had escaped from the day before, and he didn't want them to see him. So he and Crawfleece grabbed a spot under a bridge, close enough to hear and peek over.

He watched the hooded figure dozing peacefully atop the toad. Or was he dozing? Little gnomes scampered up the slippery flanks of the toad and whispered things to the figure in black. He nodded a few times, but said nothing.

The sorcerer is several hundred years old, thought Rollo, *so maybe he's conserving his energy.* It was fascinating to watch ogres, ghouls, and gnomes prostrate themselves before this mysterious being. Rollo had only seen them around trolls, when they were the masters.

Everyone in Bonespittle is a slave, Rollo realized, *to this one being—the last sorcerer.*

The giant toad was the only other creature who seemed to do exactly as he pleased. What he pleased to do was belch several times, until the ogres started feeding him slop out of buckets. It was all very interesting to the young troll. This had to be the greatest night in the history of Dismal Swamp.

Finally they had assembled enough trolls to allow the sorcerer to speak. There were trolls as far as Rollo could see, and the old bridges were sagging badly. He hoped it wouldn't be a long speech, or much of the audience would find themselves in the swamp.

At last Stygius Rex rose to his feet and stood atop the giant toad. He pushed back his hood while his minions lifted their lanterns so the trolls could see his face. Rollo gasped, as did many others. His pictures didn't do him justice. Stygius Rex had a wonderfully ravaged face, with a leer of sheer malevolence. Surely this was the way an all-powerful mage was supposed to look.

"Fellow citizens of Bonespittle," he began, which was the nicest thing trolls had been called in a long time. "I have come to you because I need your help. Everyone knows there are no finer bridge builders in all of our glorious land than the trolls. This putrid village is a testament to that."

He waved his arms joyously. "I had a dream . . . a prophetic dream. In this vision, I saw a bridge stretching across the Great Chasm. This mighty bridge will unite our land with the Bonny Woods!"

Since trolls weren't as stupid as they looked, they started to mutter and edge away from the sorcerer. Most of them could see where this was headed. When ghouls on horseback cracked their whips, the muttering died down.

Stygius Rex, however, was no longer happy. "You *will* volunteer to join my work crews. Don't worry, my ghouls and ogres will protect you from the elves and fairies. You will only be required to help us *build* the bridge, not to fight. In fact, there will be no fighting. We will extend the hand of friendship to the elves and fairies."

Now they knew he was quite mad, and some trolls began to jump off the bridges into the swamp. Rollo didn't move, because he and Crawfleece were too close to the armed ogres. Instead, he decided to try a different tact.

"Long live Stygius Rex!" yelled Rollo.

The smarter trolls took up his cheer, realizing they had to do something to get rid of the sorcerer. Cries of "Long live Stygius Rex!" echoed throughout the swamp.

This mollified the mage somewhat, and he raised his arms to quiet them. "I thank you for your well wishes, but I am determined to build this bridge. General Drool will return tomorrow to collect the volunteers. I need experienced bridge builders . . . three thousand of you. There will be glory and great rewards for those who join me in this crusade."

The trolls cheered deliriously and shouted, "Long live Stygius Rex!" But most of them were trying to figure out how to get out of it. There was a reason why there were no bridges over the Great Chasm: It would be suicide! Besides, who wanted to give the dreaded fairies and elves a chance to attack them?

"Come on, Old Belch," said the sorcerer, plopping onto the toad's back. "Let's get out of this noxious bog."

Waddling about like a great lump of leach pudding, the

toad turned in the opposite direction. With a mighty leap, it soared from one mound to another, sending trolls and ogres scattering.

"Nobody will sign up for *that*," whispered Crawfleece. "He's gone stark-raving mad."

"But it must be fun to have a giant toad," said Rollo.

CHAPTER 5

BRAVE VOLUNTEERS

"I'M GOING TO JOIN UP," DECLARED FILBUM, ONE OF THE apprentices and Rollo's best friend. He, Rollo, and Crawfleece were gathered on the banks of the swamp, under a bridge. All three of them were too excited after the sorcerer's visit to go home.

"Why?" asked Rollo in amazement.

"To get out of here," answered Filbum. "I've never seen the Great Chasm . . . or anything but this crummy swamp. I want to *see* something. *Do* something! Stygius Rex is a sorcerer—if he says he can build a bridge, then he can."

"Excuse me," said Crawfleece snidely, "but he said they were looking for *experienced* bridge builders. You're just an apprentice."

"Compared to some stupid ghoul or ogre, I'm an experienced bridge builder," said Filbum proudly. Rollo tried not to look too doubtful, because Filbum was not a very good worker. He was kind of small for a troll, too. However, he always talked about getting away from Troll Town, so maybe this decision was right for him.

"Glory and great rewards," said Filbum, his eyes sparkling with dreams. "That's what Stygius Rex said."

Crawfleece rolled her eyes. "Well the Great Chasm is wider than this swamp and deeper than all the holes in Bonespittle put together. I don't think anybody can get across it, let alone build a bridge over it."

"What are you going to do about the fairies and elves?" asked Rollo worriedly.

Filbum snorted. "That's why we have ogres and ghouls. Let them deal with the fairies. I'm not a good worker, but I'm good at looking busy."

"Yes, you're good at that," allowed Rollo. He was suddenly seized with a new worry: *What if Ludicra decides to join up?*

Filbum slapped him on the back. "Come on, Rollo, you're big and strong—they'll like you a lot. Why don't you join up with me? We'll have fun together!"

"If you do, Mother and Father will kill you," warned Crawfleece.

"Trust me, I'm not going," said Rollo quickly. He sincerely doubted whether the trolls would get any kind of glory or rewards. He was sure they would get whippings, long hours, and bad food. Because that's what trolls always got when ogres were in charge.

Later, as the young troll lay in his sleeping pit, he thought about his short life, Stygius Rex, and the Great Chasm. But mostly he thought about his beloved—Ludicra. What if she signed up for the sorcerer's work crew? He might never see her again! That would be unbearable and unthinkable.

Rollo didn't really believe that someone as selfish as Ludicra would risk her life for someone else's dream. But who knew for sure? The young troll was awake and dressed at dusk. He knew where Ludicra lived, and he would go straight to her hovel and ask her.

He slipped out the door before his mother, father, and sister were awake. To his surprise, Troll Town was utterly deserted. True, it was early in the evening, but the fire-keepers should be lighting the lamps. The vendors should be setting up their food stands, farm workers should be trudging toward the fields. No one seemed to be alive except Rollo.

Not only that, but it was raining—a cold, gloomy drizzle that matched his mood. With a shiver, the young troll hurried across a series of bridges to the mound inhabited by Ludicra and her family. What would he say, since he wasn't allowed to talk to her?

Rollo climbed down the sodden vines and roots to the

doorway of her home. Boldly, he knocked upon the weathered planks.

"Who is there?" called a frightened male voice. The door did not open even an inch.

"Is Ludicra home?" he asked simply. He'd better make sure this was her hovel before he said something really stupid.

"Who wants to know?"

"I'm a friend of hers. Is she going to her apprenticeship?"

"Not today!" snapped the voice. "She's not leaving the house today—not for a million grubs. Go away, or I'll throw you in the swamp!"

Rollo said nothing, because he had learned what he had come to find out: Ludicra was not going to join the sorcerer's band. "Have a dismal evening!" he called happily. Despite the rain and the lack of people, Rollo's heart was joyous as he climbed toward the bridge.

Or it was until he heard the clomping of hooves just above him. He stopped and froze, but it was too late. They had heard his voice.

"Hey, little troll," slurred a voice, "aren't you going to come out and see who's walking on your bridge?"

"No, I don't care. Just keep on going," said Rollo pleasantly.

"Come on out," coaxed the speaker. "We have to ask directions. All these darn bridges look the same."

Rollo shrugged his beefy shoulders. He supposed it could be difficult for strangers to find their way around Troll Town.

With a sigh of resignation, the young troll hauled himself onto the bridge.

He knew instantly that he had made a mistake . . . both in leaving his home and in showing himself to the strangers. Perched above him on a tall, black steed was the ugliest, most slobbery ghoul he had ever seen. And he was surrounded by a party of grinning ogres, all of whom held crossbows with net attachments.

"I believe we have our first volunteer," said the ghoul.

Before Rollo could even duck, three ogres fired nets at him, and he found himself ensnared. Still, he stayed on his feet, staggering a few inches, until the ogres surrounded him. With a powerful lunge, he knocked one of them off the bridge into the swamp, and the water splashed over all of them.

The angry ogres brandished clubs and smashed him about the head. "Ludicra!" he yelled, falling to his knees. "Help me!"

But no one came to his aid. No one opened a door in the village of petrified trolls. The last thing Rollo remembered before he plunged into darkness was the cackle of the ghoul.

CHAPTER 6
FELLOW PASSENGERS

T HE ACHE STRETCHED DOWN ROLLO'S HEAD INTO HIS LIPS
and chin. It turned to a weird tingling sensation, then feeling slowly returned to his mouth. Something sticky, foul, and wet was stuck to his lips and his eyelids. In fact, it was all over him. Rollo felt the weight of it crushing down.

In a panic, the young troll moved suddenly, and pain jolted along his shoulders and into his arms. Still, Rollo realized he had to breathe, and he had to get out of this smothering darkness!

With a lurch, the troll rose to his feet. His legs felt weak and rubbery, and pain continued to chase up and down his body. He almost collapsed, which was easier than swimming through this moldy sea. Finally Rollo poked his head through the soil into blessedly cold, damp air. He gasped his fill of it.

As his senses returned, Rollo heard the squeaking of wheels. He realized he was in a hay wagon, bouncing over a country road. The sky was dark and gloomy, and rain mixed with freezing sleet pummeled his face. Rollo looked around and could see hulking, shrouded figures surrounding his cart—and many more rickety vehicles beyond.

Ogres trudged along on foot or drove the wagons while the ghouls rode their horses, hunched in the rain. After a while, Rollo swore he could hear their bones rattle with each plodding step of their horses.

A groan came from beneath the youth, and he poked around with his foot until he found another squirming body. *Another volunteer,* he figured. Carts were strung out behind as far as he could see, and he realized they were full of trolls.

Smart, thought Rollo, because hay wagons wouldn't alarm the populace as would cages full of prisoners. They wanted everyone to think this was a volunteer effort, even if it wasn't. How many trolls had chosen to come, and how many were really plucked off bridges?

At least we don't have to walk to the Great Chasm, Rollo thought ruefully.

The groan sounded again, followed by a muffled expression of alarm. Rollo wasn't surprised when a confused troll popped out of the hay and stared at him—but he was surprised at who it was!

"Master Krunkle?" he whispered with alarm.

"Yes, yes . . . get your paws off me!" The grizzled troll

pushed Rollo away, then he rolled up his sleeves and looked around. "I'm going to thrash a couple of ogres!"

"Quiet down there," hissed the ghoul behind them. He rode forward, pulling back his hood to reveal his rotting, cadaverous face. "If you would prefer to walk, dragging chains behind you—"

Rollo hurriedly dragged his master back into the moldy hay. "Please keep your voice down," he whispered. "We're surrounded by them."

Krunkle snorted angrily and poked his head above the hay again. Rollo feared he would start complaining, but the old troll said nothing as the wagon lurched along.

"Where did they capture you?" asked Rollo glumly.

"At work, of course. Nobody showed up . . . and where were *you?*" The old builder muttered under his breath when he realized how stupid that question was. "Right, you were here. This is a fine bucket of worms! We show up to do our duty and get waylaid for our trouble."

"At least with you," said Rollo, "they got somebody who actually knows how to build a bridge."

Krunkle shook with rage for a moment, then he managed to hiss a reply: "That old sorcerer is crazy. He can't build a bridge across that chasm—no one can. How are you going to create it? Where are you going to stand? Where do the load-bearing supports go?"

Rollo shook his head. "Maybe he plans to use . . . magic?"

"More reason to get out of here!" rasped the old troll. He reached into the folds of his clothes and fumbled around. Rollo couldn't imagine what he was looking for, but then the builder came up with a pouch and a broad grin. "This is my emergency tool kit. I'm going to get us out of here."

"While we're moving?" whispered Rollo.

"Why not?" Krunkle burrowed down beside him. "You keep watch while I take out a few planks in the floor of this wagon. We'll slip right out the bottom and roll off into the ravine at the side of the road. They won't know they're missing two trolls, and we'll be home for supper."

"All of that sounds wonderful," admitted Rollo, "especially the part about supper. But isn't it risky?"

Krunkle snarled. "As if staying with a crazy sorcerer and an army of thugs is safe?"

"When you put it that way . . . ," Rollo gulped. "I'll keep watch."

Rollo stuck his head above the hay and tried to look nonchalant as he peered at the dark shapes trudging through the sleet. Most of them had their hoods up and their heads down, and they probably weren't paying much attention. He could hear sawing noises beneath him, and he tried to keep his feet out of the way.

After what seemed like half the night, Rollo heard wood scraping wood. It sounded as if someone were moving furniture. Then he felt a tug on his pant leg, and he ducked back under the hay.

"Careful now," cautioned Krunkle. "There's a big hole here where there used to be a wagon bed. You're sitting on the boards I removed. Drop down and roll to the right. Don't let the wheels get you."

"Yeah, the wheels," answered Rollo with a nervous gulp.

"See you later!" With those words and a muddy thud, the old builder was gone.

Did he escape? There was no way to tell unless Rollo went above and looked around . . . or followed through the hole. Rollo could see nothing in the darkness under the stifling hay, and he couldn't even open his eyes. He had to feel around with his hands.

Finally Rollo felt the rough edges of the hole, where Krunkle had sawed his way through. He could feel cold air rushing under the wagon, and it smelled like freedom. The hole felt way too small for Rollo's girth, but the young troll knew he had to try. His old master expected him to follow.

Cautiously, he swung a leg into the hole.

"No, no, don't do it!" squeaked a little voice somewhere in the darkness.

"What? Who speaks?" Rollo was quaking with fear.

"It's the voice of reason. Pause for a moment, and you will hear."

Rollo was frozen stiff with fear, so pausing came naturally. After a few moments he heard voices and shouting, followed by a muffled yell.

"You see, they've caught your friend," said the voice

matter-of-factly. "He'll be sorry he tried to escape, I'm sure of that. And now I'll have to move to another wagon—this one has a drafty hole in it."

"Wait, wait," said Rollo urgently. "Thank you for warning me. Who are you?"

"Hoist me to the top—I'm too short to get up there myself. Be careful of that stupid hole." Two stubby hands reached across the darkness and tugged on Rollo's sleeve. With his long arms, the troll picked up his fellow passenger, who felt no bigger than a child.

The troll lifted him upward through the hay, and both of them stuck their heads out. Rollo peered into the darkness behind them, trying to find his old master. He wished he hadn't looked for Krunkle, because he saw a ghoul on horseback dragging a lumpen mass behind him. Several laughing ogres ran along beside the bundle, prodding it.

With a sigh, he turned back to look at the child. Only it wasn't a child—it was a very ugly gnome with bristling hair, crooked nose and teeth, and several hairy warts. The small being had to hang on to the side of the wagon to keep from slipping back into the hay.

Rollo gulped and tried to be brave. "Did you . . . did you volunteer, too?"

The gnome laughed. "No more than you. I was sleeping peacefully a couple of days ago when the master summoned me with this grand idea. I'm the official scribe, you see. My name is Runt."

"Pleased to meet you. I'm Rollo," said the young troll. "If they'll listen to you, you might want to spare the life of my friend. He's Krunkle, the master bridge builder. He's the one who trained all the rest of us."

"Keep him alive, you say?" said the gnome, rubbing his chin thoughtfully. "The ogres won't like that, but who can please an ogre?" He pointed a stubby finger at the nearest ghoul. "You there, get me General Drool! Tell him Runt needs to speak with him. It's urgent."

The ghoul nodded, then spurred his horse to charge through the mud toward the front of the line. Rollo shivered at the mention of General Drool, who was known as the worst of a hideous race. The young troll had many questions. Where were they going? What was going to happen to them? Could they really build a bridge across the Great Chasm?

"Sir Runt," he whispered, "why were you hiding in this wagon?"

"Why do you think? To keep from having to walk." The gnome brushed straw out of his bushy hair. "I was very comfortable until your friend started making all that noise."

"Why did you let him escape, but not me?"

"Because I was listening and heard it was *his* idea. I could tell you have more sense than he does. He's the type who must have it proven to him that escape is a mistake. I hope he's learned his lesson."

The ugly gnome wagged a finger at him. "You remember that, young Rollo—we deal harshly with those who try to escape. I won't stop you if you want to take a risk, but I'll laugh like crazy when you fall on your face."

"Is that what you're doing with this bridge project?" asked Rollo innocently.

The gnome glowered at him with bristling eyebrows. "Don't get too smart, young troll. Look sharp, because here comes the general."

Plodding through the rain came a tremendous black steed, snorting steam. Astride him sat a tall, angular ghoul, whose slack mouth failed to contain a stream of saliva. "Runt, what do you want?" he slurred.

"General," said the gnome with a bow, "your troops are entertaining themselves with an old troll they captured trying to escape. Normally I wouldn't care what they did with him, but this lad informs me he's a master bridge builder. He's the one who trains the others."

For the first time, General Drool turned his attention to Rollo, who cringed from the blazing madness in his empty eye sockets. "You're not lying just to save him, are you?"

"No, sir," answered Rollo quickly. "You can ask any troll from Troll Town. They all know Master Krunkle. I'm his apprentice . . . so were many others."

"Very well. The master will want to talk to him." The ghastly ghoul yanked on his reins and galloped to the rear. After the general issued some blunt orders, the lumpy net was tossed on the back of the second ghoul's horse. The ogres roughly tied it down. With General Drool in the lead, the two ghouls rode past the wagon, headed toward the front.

As they sped past, Rollo heard a groan, and he tried to tell himself that Krunkle would be all right. In truth, he wondered whether any of them would be all right. And how long would it be until he saw his home and his family again?

How long would it be until he saw Ludicra?

With a million questions swirling in his mind, the troll turned back to the gnome. Runt waved him off with a scowl. "I can't let Drool take credit for all of this! I've got to see the master, too."

He slapped the big troll on his beefy back. "Just stay out of trouble and keep your nose dirty."

With that, the gnome let go of the side of the wagon and slid down into the hay. Rollo heard a splash and he turned to see the gnome on the ground, dashing away from the wagon. Runt had no trouble slipping out the hole in the bottom, and he ran fast for such a short-legged being.

Rollo shivered with a mixture of fear and cold, and he tried to get comfortable in the moldy hay. If he was going to survive this ordeal, he would have to be very careful. He would have to think for himself—not listen to anyone's advice. He should try to stay friendly with the gnome, if he could.

Who knew what was going to happen next?

CHAPTER 7
HOME, SWEET HOME

*R*OLLO WAS ONLY A YEAR OLD—A FAT, BALD, LITTLE TROLL *gurgling happily in his cradle. His mother rocked him with her foot; with her other foot, she mushed grubs for his dinner. Her guttural voice sang a sweet lullaby about picking leeches off her thigh to make a pie. Rollo laughed at that song, although he barely understood it.*

He had never been so happy as he was in that peaceful time, rocking back and forth, listening to his mother screech a song. Even when his sister threw a snake into his cradle and got scolded for it, the rocking didn't stop. Vulgalia just snatched up the snake and tossed it into the cook pot, never taking her foot off the cradle leg.

So it was jarring when the rocking motion suddenly stopped. Rollo called out, reaching for his mother, but she was gone. There was only chilled air and rancid straw to greet his parched cries.

When Rollo opened his eyes, his vision was assaulted by bright sunlight. He pushed away the hay and peered into the blazing light. With horror, he realized he was not in his baby cradle—but in a wagon, surrounded by ogres and ghouls! And it was daylight, dreaded daylight.

Pain surged up and down his stiff body as he struggled to get to his feet. Despite the sunshine, a shroud of gloom overcame the young troll as he remembered what had happened to him. It didn't help that hundreds of other wagons were behind them, and frightened trolls peered from each of them.

As he listened, Rollo heard the whoosh of rushing water. His eyes followed the sound until he realized that they were camped on the bank of a broad river with white-water rapids. The other side of the river was shrouded in early morning mist. It looked like a foreboding jungle over there.

In contrast, their side of the bank had been cleared, leaving lots of tree stumps and log piles. Rollo wondered if they were going to try to cross this raging river.

"That can't be the Great Chasm, can it?" called a voice. Rollo turned to see four trolls peeking above the hay in another wagon, which had just stopped near his.

"No, it's Rawchill River," claimed another troll in the neighboring wagon. "At least, I think it is."

"All you trolls, get out and line up!" bellowed an ugly ogre as he strolled between the wagons. "No talking! Just line up!"

Soon all the ogre guards took up the same chant. "No talking! Line up!" The trolls scurried out of the wagons and tried to form straight lines. It was difficult, because no one wanted to be in the front row. Finally one of the ghouls stuck a spear in the ground and drew a straight line as he rode past. Rollo and the other trolls hastened to toe the line.

Rollo looked for Filbum, Krunkle, or any other trolls he knew. Even though he spotted a few acquaintances, they all turned away in shame. After all, who wanted to admit he had been stupid enough to sign up for this mad venture? Or was stupid enough to let himself be captured? Rollo could only hope that his family had kept hiding.

The young troll craned his neck to watch the others line up around him. Maybe there weren't three thousand trolls in this gathering, but there were many hundreds of them. Plus, there had to be hundreds of ogres. Most of them wore studded black uniforms, but there were many ogres in regular clothes, too. Some of them looked confused.

The ogres were also assembled, although they were asked nicely. They got to joke and converse among themselves too; the no-talking rule applied only to trolls.

In the distance, they heard a loud, ground-shaking belch. A stench floated on the breeze, and Rollo turned toward the misty river. He realized the giant toad was being kept beside the water, out of sight. Although he was afraid of the massive creature, the young troll wanted to get a closer look at him.

It was mid-morning, with a hot sun beating down, before everyone got lined up to the ghouls' satisfaction. That was when Stygius Rex appeared, surrounded by gnomes holding a portable awning over his head. The sorcerer apparently did not like sunlight, although he had no problem making everyone else stand in it. Seen by daylight, he looked more dried and shriveled than his ghouls.

"Hello," said Stygius Rex with a fawning smile. "I thank you for volunteering for this heroic project—to build a bridge that will unite two great lands!"

"But I didn't volunteer!" shouted a voice among the trolls.

There was a hush, and Rollo nearly swallowed his tongue. He had been thinking that, but hadn't dared say it. Ogres moved through the lines, trying to find the culprit. But he was somewhere in the middle, and there were trolls as far as the eye could see.

The sorcerer puckered his lips distastefully. "No matter how you got here, you are here now. I would advise you to make the most of this opportunity. I wasn't lying about the glory and riches—you will attain them if you march with me all the way to victory."

He rubbed his hands together cheerfully. "Plus, all of you will learn new skills! If you don't know how to build a bridge, you will learn. If you don't know how to use weapons, you will learn that too. Some of you may even learn a bit of *magic*."

That got Rollo to perk up his pointed ears. Most of the trolls around him were attentive and even somewhat eager. That was one good thing about trolls: They forgave quickly and got on with life . . . and the usual hard work.

"Our first order of business is to put up tents, build barracks, and make a new town in this wilderness!" declared Stygius Rex. "No, this is not the Great Chasm. But this is where we must practice the skills we will need to build the bridge I envision."

That statement once again brought gasps of fear from the trolls. "Curse my nose, how can we build a bridge over those rapids?" shouted one of them.

The sorcerer's eyes narrowed. "I have my powers to help us. You *will* build a bridge over this river, and we will use this victory to span the Great Chasm. I would advise all of you to work hard."

Stygius Rex dabbed at his neck with a black handkerchief and whined, "We must get out of this dreadful sun! The gnomes will start digging tunnels; the ogres will put up tents. You trolls will start to split wood for lumber. I warn you to use those axes only on the logs. Anyone who refuses to work will be fed to Old Belch in his slop! Am I understood?"

"Yes," muttered the trolls in unison. After a lifetime of being abused and overworked, they knew what was expected.

The ghouls unfurled their whips, and loud cracks shattered the peaceful morning. Ogres, trolls, and gnomes hurried about their tasks, while Stygius Rex stood motionless in the shade of his portable pagoda.

Rollo wondered if the sorcerer would stand there until they built him a city in this wilderness. Behind the troll, the Rawchill River thundered through the mist. It reminded him of the challenge yet to come.

The ogres erected rows and rows of small, ragged tents, and they promptly crawled into them and went to sleep. The gnomes burrowed underground and were seen no more. Stygius Rex soon tired of the sunlight and went underground with the gnomes. By noon, only a few ghouls patrolled a vast gathering of disgruntled trolls.

Most of the trolls kept splitting logs, but their work was slow and disorganized. Like Rollo, they were more interested in trying to find their friends and family. They roamed among the throng, looking for acquaintances while pretending to work. With so many folks pretending to work, it was difficult for Rollo to pick out his friend, Filbum.

They were allowed to get water from the river, but without buckets or tools, that was a hazardous undertaking. More than one troll fell into the swift current and was gone. *But maybe they are trying to escape,* thought Rollo. It was definitely a disheartened group, more like a prison camp than a work camp.

The only thing that kept them in line was the smell of food cooking in the tent city of the ogres. *Surely, they will feed us,* thought Rollo. As the day wore on, many of the trolls stopped working and began to look for grubs in the mud and the tree stumps.

That was when Stygius Rex reappeared, and he wasn't alone. Master Krunkle was with him, but the old builder looked dazed and slack-jawed—like one of the ghouls. Ogres cleared a path for the sorcerer and the troll, and gnomes followed with the canopy to keep them both in shade.

Upon reaching the center of the camp, the sorcerer embraced the troll like an old friend. "Hear ye! Hear ye! I am pleased to present Krunkle, the master bridge builder from Troll Town. Most of you were apprenticed to him in your youth. Master Krunkle has generously volunteered to organize our effort and lead the training. He will work directly with *me!*"

This was greeted with muttering of approval, but Rollo wasn't impressed. He pushed through the crowd in order to get a better look at his old master. It was Krunkle, all right, but the vacant look in his eyes disturbed the young troll.

In a flat voice, Krunkle said, "Now the master says it is time to eat. Hail to Stygius Rex."

A lot of hailing and cheers greeted that proclamation. Ogres took over, allowing the oldest trolls to eat first. Rollo tried to reach Krunkle to speak with him, but the masters were spirited away. Under close guard, the sorcerer and his new ally disappeared into a gnome burrow.

As one of the youngest in the camp, Rollo dutifully remained behind to eat with the last group. In the thinning crowd, he finally spotted his friend, Filbum, who waved happily.

"Rollo, you came after all!" called the short troll, dashing toward him. "I knew you would!"

"Well, I didn't exactly volunteer." Rollo glanced around for eavesdropping ogres. "They stole me off a bridge and knocked me out."

"Nonsense," said Filbum. "I'm sure it was just a misunderstanding. They've treated me great!"

Rollo rolled his eyes. "You're probably the only real volunteer."

"Like the big boss said, we're here now," insisted Filbum. Nothing could dampen his good cheer. "And it will be easy to make them think we're working."

Rollo was aghast. "It's going to be hard, dangerous work to build a bridge over this river! Not to mention the Great Chasm."

"Just stick with me," said Filbum. "The way I plan to get through this, it's not going to be hard or dangerous. I plan to be around for the glory and rewards part."

"You two! Get moving to the grub line!" bellowed an ogre, stepping toward them.

When Rollo turned around to thank him, he almost squeaked in horror. It was the captain of the guard who had tried to arrest him at the Hole in the forest. A look of recognition passed across the ogre's brutish face too, and his tusks jutted upward.

Rollo tried to blend into the crowd, but the other trolls were already fleeing from him. The captain stepped right up to Rollo, staring at him. "Well, if it isn't my favorite poacher."

With a fat finger, he punched Rollo hard in the chest. "I got chewed out because of you. The commander doesn't like wounded soldiers and broken nets with no prisoner to show for them. Didn't you want to arm wrestle with me?"

Rollo laughed nervously. "I think you must have me confused with somebody else. I don't ever arm wrestle."

"Oh, sure you do!" said Filbum excitedly. "You're the champion of our class, don't you remember?"

The big troll grimaced and tried not to strangle his friend. By now, a sizable number of ogres were gathering around them, while most of the trolls had fled. The captain bared his upper fangs and scraped them along his lower tusks. Maybe it was a smile, Rollo hoped.

"We'll have to have a new bet, of course," said the enormous ogre, moving closer. His fat belly bumped against Rollo's. "If you win, you get to live. If I win, you have an accident." The other ogres laughed their approval.

"And we get twice as much food as the others," insisted Filbum. At their grim stares, he smiled and added, "I'm Rollo's manager."

"That sounds fair," squeaked Rollo.

The captain laughed and rolled up his right sleeve. "If you wish. Believe me, food will be the least of your worries after I get finished with you. Let's find a stout tree stump." He stomped away, inspecting the nearby stumps.

"Right," chirped Rollo. A feeling of numbness slowly spread over him, and he felt petrified.

Filbum began to rub his friend's arm. "Come on, Rollo, you can take him. He's all flab . . . been eating too much homemade sludge. Please beat him, because I'd really like to live. I know . . . think of all that good food you'll win!"

Food, thought Rollo, drawing strength from his hunger. The smell of food wafted all around the camp, and his stomach was beyond growling—it was rumbling. His mouth began to water, and his powerful biceps began to contract. *Yes, I can take him.*

"Come on, troll!" called the ogre. He was seated on the ground in front of a stump, with his elbow in the center of the makeshift platform.

Rollo sat down in front of the ogre. Although he was terrified, he also felt a burst of confidence. He had been the one to suggest this contest in the forest, and he wouldn't have done that if he hadn't thought he could win. He trusted his skill and his desire. Plus, he was very good at snapping his opponents' wrists.

"What are the rules?" asked Rollo before he placed his elbow on the stump.

The ogre looked confused at the idea of rules. "Let's see, we grab each other's hands, and I break your arm. What do you mean, what are the rules?"

"When do we start?" asked Rollo. "The instant our hands

meet, or do we grasp hands and wait for someone to start us?"

"The instant we grasp hands," barked the ogre. Rollo tried not to smile, because this was what he wanted. The ogre was overconfident, and Rollo didn't want to give him a chance to test the troll's strength.

"And the contest is over when the back of the loser's hand touches the wood. Right?" Rollo looked around to make sure the other ogres were listening.

The captain laughed. "Are you sure you've done this before?"

"Yes," said Rollo pleasantly, "but I don't want to turn it into a fight or anything. We are just arm wrestling."

The ogre's beady eyes narrowed. "For now. So quit your gabbing and get your arm up here."

Rollo took a deep breath of air and tried to clear his mind. He didn't think of the pudgy ogre seated in front of him; instead, he thought of the clamps that tightened the stay ropes on a troll bridge. He thought of the cutters, saws, and tools he used every day. He thought of how his strong hands grasped these instruments and made them do his bidding. With such intent, he had to grab the ogre's hand.

The young troll placed his elbow next to the troll's and saw to his satisfaction that his hand was bigger and his forearm was longer. At his calmness, the big ogre had a momentary look of doubt. That was when Rollo grabbed his hand and bent back his wrist.

The ogre's strength finally clicked in when his hand was

just an inch above the wood. He growled and tried to twist away while Rollo put his beefy shoulder into it. With all his weight, he pinned him down, and the ogre screamed as his limp hand struck the tree stump.

Rollo quickly wrenched his hand away. His arm was throbbing with pain, but he had won!

The ogres gasped in amazement and shock. Even Filbum looked stunned at the speed of Rollo's victory. The vanquished captain was furious, and his piggy, red eyes blazed at Rollo. He jumped to his feet and reached for his sword, but he howled with pain when he turned his wrist.

Awkwardly, the ogre drew his sword with his left hand. "Now you die, you brazen troll!"

CHAPTER 8
A TRICK UP HIS SLEEVE

TWO FELLOW GUARDS BUTTED IN AND GRABBED THE BIG ogre's arm. "Captain, there's a ghoul watching us!" one of them whispered. With a scowl, the ogre put down his sword and straightened to attention. He continued to stare at Rollo while everyone else turned to look at the ghoul on horseback.

It was no less than General Drool, wrapped in his gold-trimmed cape. He prodded his horse and came closer. A dark hood protected the ghoul's repulsive face from the sun, but his slack lips seemed to twist into a smile.

"Captain Chomp," he slobbered, "I believe we said to *feed* these trolls, not make sport with them. I know this one— he gave us help last night." To Rollo's shock, General Drool pointed directly at him.

"See that he and his friend eat well," ordered the ghoul.

"In fact, I believe *twice* as much as the rest of them."

"Yes, sir," said the chastened captain. He glowered briefly at Rollo, then lowered his head.

The ghoul spurred his horse and galloped away, splattering mud on all of them. At once, the captain glowered at Rollo and clenched his fists, but a female ogre pulled him aside.

"Let it go, Chomp," said the new arrival, who was somewhat thin for an ogre. She still had muscles the size of coiled main ropes. "Remember, you've got these same trolls in defense training. Accidents always happen there."

"Yeah, that's right," said the big ogre, showing lots of tusk in his smile. He jabbed a fat finger in Rollo's chest. "Remember, I'm Captain Chomp, and I'll see you later."

Chomp stomped away, but the female ogre stayed behind for a moment. She sighed and looked at Rollo and Filbum. "My name's Weevil. I'll try to get you in my company, but it won't be easy to keep Chomp away from you. Come on, let's get you *twice* as much food as the others."

As Weevil led the way through the crowd, Filbum sidled up to Rollo. He rubbed his hands together and chortled. "See, I told you this was going to be easy. You're going to be very popular here. The general *likes* you, and now all the ogres know you too!"

"I'm so popular, I'll have the first accident," muttered Rollo. "And I'm not sure General Drool likes anybody."

Filbum still had a dreamy expression on his face. "Think, Rollo—we're going to be the first of our race to visit the

Bonny Woods. We might actually *see* a fairy, instead of hearing about them in scary stories. We're like explorers!"

"I don't want to see a fairy," whispered Rollo. "And I sure don't want to explore anyplace they live."

"Don't worry, I'll protect you!" answered Filbum with a big grin.

Master Krunkle appeared at sunset, although no one was allowed to get close to him. Ogres flanked him as he strode through the throng of trolls, picking out the ones he knew. A frighteningly tall ghoul followed this procession, having words with the trolls selected.

When the bridge builder passed them, Filbum hid behind Rollo's broad back. Rollo pressed forward to greet his old master, and he was startled again by the void in Krunkle's eyes. Then came a glint of recognition, and the old troll pointed at Rollo and muttered, "That one." Then he moved on.

Rollo was instantly cornered by a ghoul, who dribbled on his feet. "You are a crew leader."

"A what?"

"Crew leader. This is your crew." His oozing stare took in about a dozen nearby trolls, including Filbum. "You trolls are in his crew, number ninety-three. Await orders." With a twitch and a spray of saliva, the ghoul turned and shuffled after Krunkle.

"*Your* crew?" muttered a big, grizzled troll. He gave Rollo a suspicious glare. "You look like a young tadpole to me."

Filbum broke in. "Rollo is a really hard worker, and he knows how to build a bridge. And how to arm wrestle. You want to arm wrestle him?"

"Sure!" exclaimed the old troll, rubbing his thick hands together.

"That won't prove anything," said Rollo wearily. "*I* didn't choose to be the crew leader. If you don't like it, why don't you go talk to the ghoul? I plan to do as I'm told, and get out of here alive. If you feel the same way, you'll have no problem with me."

"That sounds sensible," said an elder female in his crew. "Leave the lad be. Besides, none of *you* wants to deal with these ghouls and gnomes, do you?" They could all agree on that, and nobody else challenged Rollo's leadership. For now.

The young troll felt a dozen pairs of eyes watching him, wondering what he was going to do. Thankfully, an ogre started growling at them. "If you trolls want to have a place to sleep in the morning, you had better get busy! Get your lumber and straw, get your axes, and build a hut for your crew."

"A hut?" muttered Filbum. "No self-respecting troll sleeps in a hut! Why can't we sleep underground, like the gnomes?"

"Did you say something about *gnomes?*" growled the ogre, staring at the little troll.

"He said he wanted to see our *new homes!*" Rollo

73

answered quickly. "Please . . . crew ninety-three, let's get to work."

It was chaos most of the night, with the trolls trying to build something they almost never saw: houses. Luckily, some of them were vendors who had built food stalls on the bridges. The others were all bridge builders, who knew how to lash wood together.

With rope, straw, logs, sticks, and poles, they erected lumpen little houses to go along with the tents. By daybreak, a new town lay sprawled along the misty bank of the Rawchill River.

Rollo's crew didn't like their hut until they had smeared the walls with mud. Then they felt more at home. It was really crowded inside the structure when everyone squeezed in. But trolls were very social creatures, and most of them came from crowded hovels.

With grunting, groaning, and a few kicks, every member of the crew found enough room to curl up. *We're like one big family,* thought Rollo, *and I'm the parent.* That was a scary thought, and it made him think of his family. He missed them terribly, even Crawfleece.

So far, he had made one enemy and maybe a few friends. But who knew who was a real friend? In a place like this, it was every troll for himself. Even Runt, the gnome, seemed worried about the outcome of this venture. They could only hope that Stygius Rex knew what he was doing.

That wasn't a very comforting thought, but Rollo was

too tired to keep worrying. The sun was coming up, and he was lying directly in a sliver of sunlight that squeezed through the slats. The warmth seeped into his bones, and he felt himself drifting into dreamland.

A thunderous belch roared across the camp, causing Rollo to bolt awake. Staring into blackness, he sniffed the seamy odor of many trolls and felt a foot kick him in the knee. Then he remembered where he was—in the hut they had built. He was surrounded by his crew, number ninety-three.

A second monstrous burp blasted the air, followed by a third. A swamplike stench grew stronger with each belch, making Rollo homesick.

"We're so lucky," said Filbum, who was lying nearby. "Who else has a giant toad to wake them up?"

Rollo peered out between the slats, but he could see nothing but darkness and a few flickering lamps. An ogre strode past, barking orders: "Time to go to work! All trolls, get up! Assemble with your crew! Time to get up!"

Nobody in his hut moved. Some of the trolls were still snoring. Rollo didn't know how to get his crew going, but he knew he had to find a way.

Since he was the only one looking outside, he began to lie. "Look, here comes Old Belch, the giant toad. Oh, no! He flattened one of the huts where they refused to get up!"

"What?" asked someone sleepily.

"The giant toad is flattening the barracks!" shouted

Rollo. "Everyone outside. Save yourselves!" He leaped to his feet and ran toward the door, stumbling over as many sleeping trolls as he could.

This started a full-scale panic, and a dozen drowsy trolls staggered outside. "Quick! Get in a line!" shouted Rollo as he arranged them.

"Where's that toad?" growled the old troll. "I don't see him."

"He's gone already," whispered Rollo, "but here's an ogre instead."

An ogre was staring at them all right. It was the wiry female named Weevil, and she gave them a satisfied nod. "Your crew is the first one up. Who's the leader here?"

"I am," answered Rollo.

"Good job," she said. "I remember you—the arm wrestler. This crew will be the first to eat, and you will also get double portions. That's your reward for answering the muster and getting up fast."

After that, Rollo was something of a hero to the members of his crew. Food always made an impression on trolls, especially when they got to eat first and eat a lot. In fact, most of them had never eaten as well as they did that night. The grub line lived up to its name, with plenty of fresh grubs for everyone.

After they ate, they were ordered to go down to the misty riverbank. Trolls could work during daytime, but the ghouls and ogres didn't like sunlight. Fearfully the trolls approached the noisy rapids and the dark, choppy water. Although they were familiar with swamps and bogs, that kind of water stood still. This kind of water moved fast and swept everything with it.

Gnomes were busy putting up lanterns to light the bank and the teeming river. Most of their efforts only made the mist look thicker and more eerie. A bit downstream, several trolls were fiddling with a large crossbow on a stand. Rollo wandered down to see what they were doing.

From a safe distance, he watched them load a huge quarrel onto the crossbow. The massive arrow had a hooked point and a long rope attached to its tail. It wasn't really a crossbow, because they had to turn a crank to cock the bow. He heard one of them call the war machine a ballista.

What are they going to shoot with it? he wondered.

Rollo spotted Captain Chomp among the ogres, and he almost ran for cover. But his curiosity was too great. Besides, the light wasn't very good, and he made sure to stay in the shadows.

After a while, General Drool himself came over to inspect the weapon. He aimed the crossbow to shoot directly across the river, where there was nothing but a line of trees. Were they going to shoot a tree?

A moment later, that's exactly what they did. Captain Chomp pulled the trigger and shot the harpoon over the river, through the mist, and into the dark forest. Then two ogres pulled on the rope to see if it had caught in the trees.

Amazingly enough, the rope held firm. The ogres promptly tied their end to a stout tree trunk, and they had a lifeline stretching across the river.

"We've got to make sure the other side is secure," said Captain Chomp.

General Drool agreed, and Chomp jumped into the churning water and grabbed the rope. Hand over hand, the brave ogre pulled himself along the cable. Water swirled over his head, but he never let go. Soon Chomp disappeared in the mist and the rapids, although they could still hear him grunting.

Rollo was stricken with the fear that they would *all* have to cross the river in this fashion. Maybe they would be expected to cross the Great Chasm hanging by a rope!

He thought briefly about escaping, but then he remembered what they had done to Krunkle. Rollo still wasn't sure what had happened to his old master, but it was bad.

Two more ogres jumped into the raging water and tried to cross on the safety line. The young troll was distracted by murmurs and shouts in the crowd, and he turned to see a band of ghouls marching toward the river. Leading the way was Stygius Rex, and right beside him was Runt, the little gnome.

The young troll returned to his crew, and Filbum whispered to him, "Where have you been?"

"Never mind," answered Rollo. "But if anyone asks for a volunteer, keep your mouth shut."

It was clear that something was going to happen, and the

crowd of trolls and ogres grew quiet. Stygius Rex looked more serious than he had before. In fact, he looked as if he were deep in thought, paying no attention to his frightened subjects.

General Drool walked up to Runt and leaned down to speak to the gnome. Runt turned to look downstream, then nodded with satisfaction. He must have been pointing out the safety rope, thought Rollo.

Runt spoke up, "Hear ye! Hear ye! We are gathered here on the banks of the Rawchill River to witness a miracle. Our noble master, Stygius Rex, will do what no one has done in two hundred years! Using his own magical power, he will cross the Rawchill River."

The gnome sounded doubtful, and he quickly added, "This will prove to you that it can be done. In this way, we will build the bridge to the Bonny Woods!"

"Nobody can get across that wild river," whispered Filbum.

"I just saw three ogres do it," answered Rollo.

Filbum blinked at him, but the tall troll was watching the sorcerer. His arms were crossed, and his eyes were closed; he was shrouded in his usual black robes. At first, it didn't look as if Stygius Rex was doing anything, except that he did seem to get taller.

Then Rollo noticed that his feet were dangling above the ground. He grabbed Filbum and shook him. "Look, he's flying!"

"What?" The short troll stood on his tiptoes to get a better look. Sure enough, the sorcerer elevated slowly above the stunned crowd. Even Runt looked properly amazed.

There were gasps as the sorcerer extended his arms and started to float over the churning river. He dropped slowly until his feet were only inches above the water, and he looked like a black sailboat as he disappeared into the fog.

"Is that real?" asked Filbum.

"You saw it, didn't you?" said Rollo. The young troll was thrilled and excited because he finally understood. "That's how we're going to build the bridge. Magic! He'll *fly* us across."

Filbum whistled through his buck teeth. "You don't have to worry about me volunteering for that."

A moment later, Stygius Rex returned. When he landed on the bank, he staggered a bit, and General Drool had to catch him. Rollo couldn't see the sorcerer's face, but his stooped posture made it clear that he had been exhausted by his effort. The ghoul escorted him to a tree trunk, where Stygius Rex sat down.

There came spontaneous applause and cheering. No troll had thought that he would ever see the great sorcerer, much less watch him perform a magical act. *This is more than a trick,* thought Rollo; *it's something wonderful!*

After a while, the sorcerer recovered. He talked to Runt, and the little gnome strode in front of the crowd.

"Now," announced Runt, "our master will perform this same feat with a selected group of volunteers! These volunteers have been tested and certified. Of course, only Stygius Rex can cast the actual spell."

Rollo pressed forward, not wanting to miss a thing. Now he was glad that he had been trollnapped, because he could never hope to see anything like this again.

Six volunteers stepped forward: two ghastly ghouls, two smug gnomes, and two fat ogres. Of course there were no trolls in this carefully selected group. Rollo was a little disappointed in this, but he understood.

Stygius Rex rose to his feet, looking very serious. He raised his arms and pointed toward the six volunteers; he seemed to be mustering his power.

Nothing happened for a long time. Finally, the two ogres and one of the ghouls lifted a few inches off the ground. Stygius Rex waved his hands, and they soared over the wild, cold river.

At once the two ogres panicked and starting kicking their feet and screaming. They dropped like stones into the water and bobbed under like apples. Seeing this, the ghoul began to panic, too. He tried to run in stiff-legged ghoul fashion, but his feet only swayed over the water.

Stygius Rex let out a cry, and the ghoul dropped into the turbulent waves. At the sight of this disaster, the crowd erupted in muttering and wails. Rollo ran to the bank and looked downstream. He saw the two ogres clinging to the lifeline, but the ghoul was nowhere to be seen.

People shouted from the bank, and the two ogres began

to feel around in the water for the ghoul. They finally located him on the bottom and dragged him to the surface. With great effort, the trio pulled themselves to the bank.

The ogres were nearly dead, but the ghoul seemed clean and refreshed from his bath. He was so clean that none of the other ghouls would get near him.

Rollo wondered why the gnomes hadn't flown at all. Maybe they were too rooted to the ground. Whoever decided to put that safety line across the river had been thinking ahead. It had saved lives, except in the case of the ghoul, who was already dead.

The young troll looked back to see Stygius Rex faint into the arms of General Drool. He and another ghoul picked up the sorcerer and carried him away, with Runt dashing ahead of them.

Ogre guards started pushing and shoving the trolls as if they didn't want them to see what was happening. But it was too late—all of them had seen the magic fail.

CHAPTER 9

FOR YOUR OWN PROTECTION

"ATTENTION!" SHOUTED THE BIG OGRE. CAPTAIN CHOMP strode in front of a long line of trolls, who struggled to stand like soldiers. Chomp's fur was still wet from having dragged himself back across the river after the failure of the flying spell. He was in a nasty mood.

"Suck in that gut! Stick out that chin! No, not your *tongue*—your chin!" Chomp jabbed one recruit in the stomach and slapped another on the head. He went down the line, finding fault with each one.

This time, Rollo stood as far in the back row as possible. Even Filbum was farther up. The last thing he wanted was for Chomp to see him—it was better he should fade into the crowd. Other ogres were standing by, and Rollo hoped they would be divided up for training.

Maybe he would get the nice one, Weevil.

Chomp scowled. "Just because we had a small mishap tonight doesn't mean you don't have to work. Many hours of darkness are left, and we'll use them for training. I know trolls are cowardly and don't fight, but this is self-defense. For your own protection."

He snorted and wiggled his tusks in distaste. "I don't need to tell you how *wicked* the elves and fairies are. They make a ghoul seem like a cuddly warthog. The fairies are full of vile magic, and the elves are brutal murderers. They collect troll heads and use them for target practice with poisoned arrows!"

A shudder ran up and down the line. Rollo wanted to ask how they knew this, since no one had seen an elf or fairy in centuries. And why would they need poisoned arrows for target practice? But he kept his mouth shut and his head down.

"Fairies have wings," said the ogre, "so they can fly without magic. They may disrupt the building of the bridge." He stopped in front of a squat troll with a big nose. "You! What will you do when you see a fairy?"

"Scream and run," said the troll sensibly.

"No!" snapped Chomp. "You will take your weapon . . . I mean, your axe . . . and you will *bash* that fairy. Understood?"

"What if I don't have an axe?" said the troll worriedly. "What if they use magic?"

"Then you will use your *fists*." Chomp looked down at

the troll and scowled. "Listen, you're a big troll, and this is a teensy-weensy fairy. Even if they turn *you* into a dung heap, your friends can attack. There are a lot of you stupid trolls! If you all band together, you can defeat any enemy."

If we all band together, thought Rollo, we can defeat any enemy? It made sense, although he had never heard anybody say it before.

"Don't dwell too much on what happened tonight," warned the captain. "I've worked for Stygius Rex for a long time, and he doesn't give up when he wants something." Did Rollo imagine it, or did the fat ogre shiver at those words?

"Now for your training assignments," said the captain of the guard. He looked around for something, didn't find it, and growled. "Runt? Where is that lazy gnome?"

From a hole in the ground, the gnome crawled out, muttering under his breath. The dirt-covered scribe scuttled forward, waving a scroll in his hand. "Hold your hobnails, I'm coming! Really, it's been an awful night."

The gnome cleared his throat and looked at his paper. With a sigh, he began to read, "Crews one through nine will go with Captain Chomp. Crews ten through nineteen with Lieutenant Gristle, twenty through twenty-nine with Lieutenant Weevil."

Runt droned on, and Rollo worried until the gnome said, "Crews ninety through ninety-nine—" The young troll's pointy ears perked up. "You go with Sergeant Skull."

Sergeant Skull, thought Rollo. He looked at Captain Chomp and saw that the big ogre was smiling.

Sergeant Skull wasn't named correctly, because, in fact, he was missing the top of his skull. Where he should have had a pate, there was a huge metal bowl that had been sewn onto his head. This crude operation looked as if it had happened a long time ago, because folds of mottled skin had grown around the metal.

The gnarled ogre appeared to be ancient. He had gray streaks in his matted fur, and his tusks were brittle and cracked. He shuffled as he walked, and he carried an axe handle, which he slapped against his leg.

Rollo stood before Skull with about a hundred other trolls, and they were all shaking with fear. Three more ogres stood nearby with smirks on their faces. There was an axe handle lying at Rollo's feet, but he was afraid to touch it until ordered.

"Me Sergeant Skull," the ogre announced in a raspy voice that sounded like one of Old Belch's burps. "And you . . . miserable, swamp-sucking slugs!"

He spit through his aged tusks. "We should let fairies turn you into daffodils. But our orders say train you to fight. Maybe you can hold off fairies and elves until brave ogres get there.

"Pick up your weapon." The sergeant hefted his axe handle and waved it around. "Go ahead. Just a stick of wood. If you no have a club, raise your hand. My helpers give you one."

It took a few minutes for everyone to be armed with an axe handle, a club, or something. The sergeant nodded with satisfaction. "We learn to parry first. Parry means blocking attack. If they attack you, you must stay alive. Need trolls to build bridge."

Sergeant Skull grabbed the three trolls closest to him and pulled them out of line. "I turn my back on you slugs. You come after me with clubs. Plan your attack. If you hit me, I let all trolls go to dinner."

That sounded like a great deal, and all the trolls began to whisper encouragement to their chosen fellows. Skull turned around as he promised and let his club dangle at his side. The three trolls looked frightened but also determined. It wasn't often that an ogre invited three trolls to hit him.

In urgent whispers, the trolls discussed what to do. Rollo noticed the other ogres were laughing among themselves. Maybe they knew how this was going to come out.

Filbum turned to him, grinning. "I sense an early dinner."

"Don't count on it," answered Rollo.

The three trolls whirled around, looking determined. One of them ran in a circle toward Sergeant Skull's face, and the other two charged his rear. Rollo thought this was a wise plan, because Skull would be distracted by the attacker right in front of him. He might miss the two at his back.

As the lead troll closed in, swinging his club, Skull ducked low and grabbed him by the arm. He hurled the poor troll over his back into his fellows, and the three attackers ended up in a squirming pile.

Skull whirled around and motioned to them. "Get up, you pond-sucking scum!"

That got the trolls enraged, and they leaped to their feet to rush the old ogre. Gripping the axe handle by both ends and using the middle to parry, he fended off blow after blow. Then Skull crouched low and whacked their skinny knees with one swing of his club.

All three trolls dropped to the ground, clutching their knees and moaning. All around Rollo, the recruits muttered in shock and alarm.

"I like to strike low," explained Skull. "Enemy not get far on stumps for legs. But go low, you risk attack on head." Gingerly, the grizzled ogre touched the metal bowl on top of his head, as if the memory of that blow was still fresh.

"Now find a partner," said the sergeant. "We practice parry."

Whacking and clacking sounds echoed through the night as the trolls parried with their clubs. Mixed in with the thwacking sounds were meaty thuds and yelps of pain when some trolls missed. Rollo started practicing with Filbum, but he hit the shorter troll too often on the head. So he switched to another member of his crew, a tall adult named Slimetoe.

This was the kind of sport that Rollo liked—he was big and strong and had quick reflexes. In fact, the young troll had to go easy on Slimetoe. When they finally took a break, every troll was exhausted and had smashed knuckles.

"Attacking more easy," declared Skull in his raspy voice. "Just split something. Split knee, split head, split chest . . . all good."

The trolls practiced attacking and parrying for hours, until they were all severely beaten. When Skull finally ordered them to stop, the sun was starting to rise over the scrubby hills to the east.

"Tomorrow war games," he promised with a grin on his sagging face. "Go eat, be strong."

After the thrilling exercise and big dinner, Rollo felt tired but happy. Still, he was troubled about the reason behind all of the activity. Somewhere across the seething river and the barren plains was the real enemy—the Great Chasm.

Maybe the elves and fairies didn't want a bridge to their Bonny Woods. Maybe they didn't want to visit Bonespittle either. In fact, since fairies could fly, they could have gone to Bonespittle anytime they wanted.

Rollo wanted to know why this was so important to Stygius Rex. The sorcerer was the key, because nobody else wanted the bridge. He had never thought about the leadership of Bonespittle before. Stygius Rex had been nothing but a picture hanging on the wall. Now Rollo saw how much power the sorcerer had over their lives.

Most of the trolls, like Filbum, were not complaining. They enjoyed eating well and seeing someplace new. But Rollo had a bad feeling that the good times were about to end.

CHAPTER 10
WAR GAMES

WHEN THE TOAD BELCHED THE NEXT EVENING, ROLLO'S crew jumped up and rushed out of their shack. Once again, they were expecting to eat first as a reward for their hustle. They were met by stern-faced ghouls and ogres, who forced them into tight lines.

As soon as the other huts emptied, all the trolls were herded down to the river. Rollo dreaded another trip to the icy rapids, but Filbum was happy as usual.

"What do you think they'll have for breakfast?" he asked. "Poached lizards with leech dip?"

"First we'll have some magic," answered Rollo, gazing down at the dense fog over the water. "I hope they make it across this time."

"Don't worry about the boss," said Filbum. "He knows

his stuff. Did you see the way he flew out over that river? Nerves like iron."

"But he was the only one who made it," whispered Rollo. He looked around at the teeming mass of trolls, some sullen, some happy, most resigned to their fate. "His plans will need a *lot* of magic."

"Quiet there!" growled a grumpy ogre. Although he wasn't really shouting at Rollo, the young troll clammed up.

In short order, they were again arrayed at the riverbank. Rollo gazed downstream to make sure the safety line was still stretched across the frigid water. It was, and trolls were stationed on the bank. He assumed trolls were also on the other side of the rapids.

Rollo didn't even want to think about being dragged by the current into that cold, foggy darkness.

A hush fell upon the gathered minions. Rollo stood on tiptoe to look over the heads and pointed ears. He saw Runt first, followed by General Drool, then Stygius Rex himself. Four very brave ogres stationed themselves at the water's edge, and Captain Chomp was one of them.

There was no point in announcing what they were going to do. It was obvious from the grim look on the sorcerer's face. He was going to fly these four ogres across the river or give them their first bath in years.

"Good food *and* entertainment!" whispered Filbum with a chuckle.

When Stygius Rex raised his arms, Rollo almost covered

his eyes. But he had to watch, if just to see what happened to Captain Chomp. It would be handy if the big ogre were washed away in the churning rapids, but he couldn't wish that on anyone.

Three of the four ogres started to rise into the air, and Captain Chomp was the only one left on the ground. He hopped a few times, trying to keep up with them, but it was no good. *Just too fat,* thought Rollo. *Too much homemade sludge.*

At first, things went well. The three ogres levitated over the water and didn't panic. When the mist swirled around them, they began to dip toward the rapids. But Rollo recalled that Stygius Rex had also dipped toward the water when he flew across.

Now the wizard stood on the foggy bank, moving his arms like a puppeteer. From the deep frown on his ashen face, it was clear that he was working hard. The ogres continued to drop lower.

When the waves lapped at their feet, that was too much for two of the ogres. They began to shout and claw the air, as if trying to climb invisible ladders. Down they came, splashing into the frenzied rapids.

The lone survivor closed his eyes and didn't seem to be panicking. Nevertheless, his progress faltered, and he just hung in the air like an especially ugly lantern. He couldn't go forward or come back.

The sorcerer finally waved his hand with disgust, and

the third ogre plummeted into the water. Stygius Rex looked disgruntled, but at least he hadn't fainted. He conferred briefly with Runt and General Drool, then he retreated into a hole in the ground.

Captain Chomp looked embarrassed by his failure to even get off the ground. He rushed to the lifeline to make sure that his fellow ogres made it to safety.

Soon the guards ordered the workers into the tent city for breakfast, which was fine with them. The mood of the trolls was very cheerful as they marched along. Here they were, about to eat another good meal, and the dangerous part of their job had been delayed again.

Although he still worried about his family, Rollo got caught up in the tide of joy. Maybe they could eat well for a few days, watch a failure that wasn't their fault, then go home. Compared to the Rawchill River, the swamps of Troll Town seemed wonderful.

After breakfast, Rollo, Filbum, and the other members of their crew went to the training field. What they found were piles and piles of empty flower pots. These were medium-size clay pots—some red, some brown. All were painted with crude yellow stripes.

Rollo's heart sank, because he was certain they would have to spend the rest of the night gardening. Just when this adventure was starting to get interesting, it was back to boring work.

Sergeant Skull laughed at their grim faces. "Oh, no—you not dig in dirt. You soldiers now! Not trolls. Put on those helmets."

Helmets? thought Rollo with confusion. All he saw were flower pots.

Filbum picked up one of the clay containers and yanked it over his floppy ears. He straightened the pot and slapped it down tightly. "Hey!" he said with delight. "It fits pretty good!"

In amazement, Rollo picked up one of the empty pots. He tried to pull it over his head, but it was too small. After looking around, he found a larger flower pot that fit nicely. Plus, it had a small hole in the top, which let in some air. Otherwise, wearing a flower pot could get very hot, Rollo discovered.

He looked around and saw a hundred other trolls who looked just as silly as he did. *Okay, we have our clay helmets. What's next?*

"Get your weapons!" growled Skull. Rollo knew what this meant, and so did the others. They rushed to the pile of axe handles, and each one found a beat-up club from the night before.

"Form ranks! Present arms!" ordered the sergeant. There was a quick inspection, and Skull and his helpers made sure that every troll in the company was armed with a handle and a flower pot.

The grizzled old ogre looked satisfied. "I promised you war games. This is mock combat—like scum stew with no bugs. Flower pot is your head. When enemy break it, you dead."

With hairy knuckles, he rapped his own metal dome. "Take care of your head! Use your brain. For pride of this out-fit, you must win. Forward march!"

Filbum was beaming with excitement as they marched into the darkness, but Rollo wasn't so thrilled. He was pretty sure that someone would be swinging an axe handle at his head. He would have to parry for real, or they might break his skull along with the flower pot.

Finally they reached a well-lit field of scrub brush and jagged cactus. Ogres, ghouls, and gnomes surrounded them, holding lanterns. Rollo realized that these observers formed the boundary of the arena. In the distance he could see a sim-ilar mob of trolls arrayed against them. They had red stripes painted on their helmets.

The two armies in flower pots sized each other up. *Are they as nervous as I am?* wondered Rollo. Probably.

"Our banner!" shouted a raspy voice. Rollo turned to see Sergeant Skull plant a pole in the earth; a ragged yellow flag fluttered from it.

"Enemy has red flag!" he explained. "You get their flag before they get ours." The old troll's rheumy eyes narrow, and he hissed, "Skull no like to lose."

Gnomes hustled in front of them, and they repeated the rules. A broken flower pot meant you were dead and had to come out of the game. Rollo could imagine that many trolls were planning to break their own flower pots. That way, they could get out of this crazy contest before they got hurt.

But not him. For some reason, he wanted to prove himself to these smug ogres and gnomes. They didn't think that trolls could fight, but Rollo had met plenty of tough trolls. In the swamp, they had to fight snappers and suckers with their bare hands.

"Rollo, what are you going to do?" asked Filbum nervously.

The young troll shrugged his beefy shoulders. "I don't know."

"Crews ninety-six through ninety-nine, stay in reserve to guard flag," ordered Sergeant Skull. "The rest of you—attack!"

"I guess we're going to attack," said Rollo.

"Not me," whispered Filbum, backing away. "I just promoted myself to crew ninety-nine. Sorry."

"Ready?" called a gnome. "At the signal, attack." He lifted a bony horn to his lips, and Rollo felt like he had worms squirming in his belly. The thought made him hungry, but he was so afraid.

It's just another game, he told himself. *You've done stupider things than this, like swinging on a vine over the Hole.*

The gnome blew his horn, which made an awful bleating sound. Sergeant Skull screamed, "Charge!"

At once, the trolls erupted with frightened muttering. Some of them rushed forward, others shuffled cautiously, and a few ran in the opposite direction. But there was really no place to hide on the barren plain. Everyone was going to have to parry or get their noggin busted.

Rollo stood still, because a plan was hatching in his mind. It was really a rather sneaky plan, the kind his sister might come up with.

He ran back to his friend, Filbum. "Come on!" he shouted. "Get on my shoulders!"

"What?" asked the little troll.

"You sit on my shoulders, and you'll be so tall that no one can bust your helmet."

Now Filbum understood, and his eyes widened with delight. Whacking and crushing sounds already echoed through the night as the lines clashed in battle. There was no time to lose!

Rollo crouched down, and Filbum jumped onto his shoulders, wrapping his legs around the bigger troll's head. With a grunt, Rollo rose to his feet, and he was suddenly a giant. Not only was Filbum's head out of reach, but both of them could use their clubs to protect Rollo's flower pot.

This lumbering giant waded into battle with twin clubs swinging. If an enemy parried Rollo's blow, Filbum got him, and vice versa. The giant smashed clay pots right and left, sending dozens of enemy trolls to the sidelines. With Filbum protecting his head, Rollo could stay on the attack.

"Look out! On your left!" shouted Filbum, who was also a second pair of eyes. With both of them working together, they were devastating. The other trolls on the yellow team rallied around the giant for protection, and Rollo was soon leading the attack.

It was all a strange kind of blur. Rollo felt as if he were circling above the mock battle, watching it from afar. He could see ogres on the other team, ordering the red soldiers to attack him directly. But it was no use, because he had a phalanx of protectors now. The battle was raging around him, yet Rollo made steady progress toward the red flag.

His fear was gradually replaced by determination. Rollo could see the enemy flag in the corner of the field. He didn't know what was happening behind him, but the goal was in sight! Smashing two more enemy flower pots, Rollo lurched toward the prize.

"That's *cheating!*" an ogre yelled as he jumped up and down on the sidelines. "That yellow troll is cheating!"

"Ignore him," said Filbum. "We're almost there!"

With victory in their grasp, the yellow team went into a frenzy. Rollo hardly had to do anything—he was swept along in a mad rush of thwacking clubs and broken pottery. Red team defenders scrambled for the sidelines, glad to escape from the massacre of flower pots.

Now the red flag was within arm's reach, and the trolls parted to let the giant have the honor. With a howl of victory, Filbum leaned over Rollo's head and snatched the tattered red cloth. They were mobbed by joyous victors, and Filbum was dragged off Rollo's shoulders.

Laughing and slapping one another on the back, dozens of trolls tumbled into a pile. Rollo was at the bottom, but he was the happiest one of all.

"Attention!" growled several ogre voices. The pile began to fall apart, and Rollo was finally able to stagger to his feet.

The first thing he saw was Sergeant Skull, who was grinning like a real skull. "Well done!" he said, looking straight at Rollo. "Good use of brain."

"He was cheating!" snapped a familiar voice. Rollo turned to look, and the smile drained from his rubbery face. Glaring at him was Captain Chomp, and he was wearing a red sash. "*You!* I should have known it was *you,* the trouble-making poacher!"

"He no cheat," countered Skull. "No rule against that. This troll smart. You owe me a jar of sweet-and-sour tapeworms."

The irate captain paid no attention to the old warrior. He was too busy glaring at Rollo. "You've shown me up for the last time."

"Let it go, Chomp," said another voice. Rollo turned to see the female ogre, Weevil, come striding into their midst. "You haven't figured it out yet, but this is a special troll."

"Oh, he's special all right," muttered Chomp. "And I've got a special assignment for him and his crew." With a glint in his piggy eyes, the big ogre stomped away.

CHAPTER 11
ONCE A HERO

"**D**ID YOU SEE HOW OUR GIANT CRUSHED THEIR NOGGINS?" shouted Slimetoe with a snorting laugh. Crew ninety-three were all lying down in the hut, but no one was asleep. "That two-headed monster just cut through them like leeches through fur!"

The hut shook with cheers and applause, and Rollo was slapped on the back once again. He wanted to tell them to settle down and go to sleep, but they were too excited. The grayish-pink sky showed that daylight was on its way, but nothing was brighter than the glow of their victory.

"How many pots did the giant break?" asked a troll named Mildewy, the oldest female in the group.

"I don't know, how many did we get, Rollo?" said Filbum. "What would you say, thirty or forty?"

"Not that many," answered the big troll with a smile. "Now all of you need to go to sleep."

"And the way that big ogre looked fit to pop!" said Slimetoe with a hooting laugh. "He said you showed him up before, Rollo. What happened then?"

"It's a long story. If you go to sleep, I'll tell you in the evening." Rollo stretched, feeling all of his muscles ache at the same time.

"Yeah, let's go to sleep," said Filbum with a yawn. "That's what the boss wants."

The boss, mused Rollo. *This time, he isn't talking about Stygius Rex—he's talking about me!*

The young troll had barely closed his eyes—or so it seemed—when the flap over the door flew back and sunlight pounded in. Everyone muttered and groaned as they tried to shield their eyes from the blaze, but there was no escape.

"Who wakes us up in the middle of the day?" muttered Mildewy.

A tall shadow darkened the doorway. "It is I, General Drool. Assemble outside at once."

When they heard the sound of a whip crack, they really began to move. Squinting into the sunlight, which was low in the west, crew ninety-three stumbled into line.

When Rollo looked around, he was shocked to see how many dignitaries awaited them. There was the gnome, Runt, plus several ogres, including Chomp and Weevil. Presiding over all of them was General Drool, whose face was mostly hidden by his hood.

"Hello again," said Runt, glancing at Rollo. The gnome cleared his throat and frowned importantly. "You and your crew have been chosen for a great honor. A great honor indeed!"

Suddenly Rollo had a sinking feeling in his stomach.

"Yes, you will be the first trolls to have the honor of *flying* across the Rawchill River. Then later you will soar across the Great Chasm, borne by the magic of Stygius Rex!"

"Oh, no!" Filbum fainted dead away.

Rollo didn't faint, but he was forced to glance at a grinning Captain Chomp. "I suggested you," said the fat ogre, "seeing as how you bested my company last night. And seeing how much *help* you've been to all of us."

"We need an intelligent troll for this," said Runt darkly. "You're the one, Rollo. And of course your friends too."

"But," squeaked Rollo, "I thought only ogres and ghouls were fit for such magic."

"We thought so, too," answered General Drool, spraying him with a putrid mist. "But they weren't so good at it."

The ghoul leaned toward Rollo, his decayed face looking like a skinned gator. "This is your chance to raise the honor of all trolls. Flying is not impossible—the master has sent me aloft many times. You must conquer your fear."

Runt hopped over to Rollo and peered up at the big troll. "Let's do this properly, all right?" begged the gnome. "So we won't have to get up so early."

"You can do it," said Weevil with encouragement. "It's concentration, that's all."

"Then why don't *you* do it?" asked Rollo.

"Are you crazy? I'd drown." She laughed heartily and pounded Rollo on the back. "Come on, there's only an hour before sunset, and you may eat a small amount."

Filbum sat up and shook his head. "A small amount? *Things* are getting worse."

Things were getting worse, all right. The biggest change was that Rollo was no longer a hero to the rest of his crew—he was an outcast. No one would sit with him during breakfast, not even Filbum. Even the ogres stayed away, except for the cook and Weevil, who made sure they didn't eat too much.

The trolls of crew ninety-three ate like condemned prisoners, silently picking at their food. It was finally more than Rollo could stand. He slammed down his bowl and banged his fist on the table.

"Listen to me," said Rollo, "I know you're all mad at me, and you're afraid. I'm afraid, too. But maybe this *is* a great honor."

They stared at him as if he were crazy, but Rollo went on. "We're trolls—we've gone through life trying to stay under the bridge. Stay out of sight. We didn't want anyone to notice us. Well, they have noticed us. They want us to do something special, something that all their ogres and ghouls and gnomes can't do."

Now the trolls were listening; they even stopped eating. "Haven't you ever felt like you could *fly?*" said Rollo wistfully. "Haven't you looked at the crows and dragonflies and wondered what that's like? I have. And I know we can do it.

"If you watched the others try it, you saw the same thing I did. The ones who flew over the water were doing fine, until they started to panic. I think they were afraid of the water, but we've been around water all our lives. I didn't see any snappers or suckers in that river."

The others laughed nervously, and Rollo added, "If you panic, you make it hard for Stygius Rex to keep you in the air. If you relax and just float along, it's easy for him. He could probably fly you all the way to Troll Town.

"You know," whispered Rollo, "they're going to make us do this, whether we want to or not. You know they expect us to fail. So let's prove them wrong! The worst that can happen is that we get a cold bath. The best that can happen is that we're heroes!"

The young troll gazed from one droopy face to another. "The question is, are you going to stay under a bridge all your life? Or are you going to do something brave and important?"

"Okay," said Slimetoe, looking sheepish. "If this young tadpole says we can do it, we'll do it. Let's show them that trolls are just as good as anyone else!"

The others muttered in agreement, although some still sounded doubtful. Filbum shook his head in amazement. "Rollo, you could sell swamp water in Troll Town."

*　　　*　　　*

Rollo and his crew were already at the riverbank when thousands of trolls and ogres gathered to watch. The audience looked more horrified than the subjects. They must have figured that if Stygius Rex was now using trolls, then nobody was safe.

Filbum was already acting like a hero as he smiled and waved to the crowd. Rollo waited patiently, telling himself not to be afraid. *I'm going to fly*, he kept repeating in his mind. He scanned the crowd for Stygius Rex, but of course the great sorcerer would have to make a grand entrance.

Finally there came a procession of gnomes and ghouls, led by Runt and General Drool. Not far behind them came the famed sorcerer, looking somber and grim. He walked up to Rollo's crew and looked curiously at them, as if he had never seen a troll before.

Most of them turned away from Stygius Rex's piercing eyes, but Rollo looked directly at him. He could see so much wisdom in the sorcerer's haggard face—but also cruelty and cunning.

"You're not afraid?" asked the mage, gazing directly at Rollo.

"No, sir," squeaked the young troll. "I'm going to *fly*."

"Indeed you are. You will fly into history." Stygius Rex waved his arms and lowered his head. "Quiet, everyone, while I concentrate."

With a gulp, Rollo turned to look at the churning river,

with its cold layer of fog. He could swear there were chunks of ice floating in the Rawchill River. The young troll whispered to his crew, "Remember, we can do this. Let's all hold hands."

He gripped Filbum's hand, and Mildewy gripped Filbum's hand. The dozen trolls stood in a circle, holding hands like children. Rollo could feel the strength of his fellow trolls, and he knew they were a noble race. They had once been a mighty race, according to his father.

The young troll wasn't sure how long they stood there, shivering in the darkness, but he felt a strange lightness in his stomach. He glanced toward the aged wizard. Stygius Rex's eyes were rolled back in his head, and his mouth formed strange, guttural sounds. With a jerk, the sorcerer threw his arms skyward.

At that same moment, Rollo's feet lifted off the ground. He gripped the hands of those around him, trying to pull all of them with him. "We can do it," he said aloud. "We trolls can do anything we want."

Although Rollo had never flown before, the sensation was more thrilling than scary. He felt as if he were swinging on a vine over the Hole, only the vine was invisible. The cold air whipped against his face, and the rapids splashed against his feet, but he didn't panic.

He was flying, and it was wonderful!

Rollo sensed that some of his crew were not so thrilled. He caught sight of the pale moon overhead; wispy clouds were drifting across it. "Look up," he said. "That's all we are: clouds floating across the face in the moon."

With mist all around them, it was easy to believe they were clouds. As his comrades gazed at the moon, he felt their confidence growing. There were cheers coming from the audience on the bank, and that encouraged them even more. Soon, the flock of trolls was soaring over the choppy waves, picking up speed.

Filbum squealed with laugher, and Slimetoe hooted excitedly. They weren't just floating—they were zooming!

All too quickly, Rollo felt the crunch of earth under his feet. Everyone in the group was surprised at their sudden landing, and they collapsed into a squirming pile. The trolls grabbed their clothes and one another to make sure they were still dry, and they were!

They looked around and saw two amazed ogres, holding lanterns. Other than that, there was nobody in sight. They were on the far side of the river!

"We made it!" cried Filbum.

"Oh, that was easy," chirped Mildewy. "When can we do it again?"

"I told you that trolls could fly," said Slimetoe smugly.

The cheers from the other side of the river were loud and frenzied. Every troll in camp was celebrating the feat. One of the ogres on Rollo's side marched up to them, and he had such a look of shock on his face that Rollo almost didn't recognize him.

It was Captain Chomp. For the first time ever, he was speechless as he stared at the young troll. Rollo was so happy that he grabbed the fat ogre in a joyous hug; Chomp was so stunned that he didn't even fight back.

"We did it!" cried Rollo. "You had faith in us!"

"I did?" asked Chomp in amazement. He scratched a curled tusk and snorted. "That's right, *I* picked you. Maybe I'll get a promotion."

"You deserve it!" said Rollo happily.

The big ogre shook his head and muttered, "Looks like I was wrong about you, young poacher. You *are* kind of special for a troll."

"And you're kind of special for an ogre," said Rollo happily.

CHAPTER 12
A SCOUTING EXPEDITION

STYGIUS REX WAS SO PLEASED WITH HIS BAND OF FLYING trolls that he sent over a large tent and lots of food. Rollo and his crew were invited to stay on the other side of the river—in a new camp. The sorcerer announced that those trolls who volunteered to fly would receive special treatment.

That night, crew ninety-three feasted and partied while the other trolls were put to work making bridge planks. Chomp and the ogres waited on them hand and foot. It was heaven, and the young troll was sad to see the night end.

In the glow of his success, Rollo's fears were fading. Now he believed they actually *could* build a bridge across the Great Chasm. And if the stupid elves and fairies didn't like it, fie on them.

Rollo went to sleep, dreaming about the glory that was Bonespittle.

For the second day, the flap over the door flew open, and sunlight shot into the dwelling. The trolls muttered and groaned, then they remembered that they were important. If Bonespittle needed them, they would wake up in the middle of the day.

An ominous figure darkened the doorway, and Filbum said, "General Drool! Do you need us?"

"Not you. Just Rollo," he hissed.

"But we're a team," insisted Filbum.

"Rollo, outside." The ghoul dropped the tent flap and was gone.

"I'll be back soon," said Rollo, scrambling to his feet. "I hope."

"Save us some food!" called Filbum.

Squinting and covering his eyes, Rollo staggered out the door into the sunlight. He didn't know who would welcome him this morning, and he was a little disappointed to see only two people. Both wore dark hoods, and he wasn't sure which one was General Drool. He figured the second one was another ghoul.

"I'm here, General." Rollo heard a whinny, and he turned to see three horses, who were dripping wet.

"Good," answered the ghoul. "Can you ride a horse?"

The troll shrugged. "I don't know, I never tried."

"If you can fly, you can ride," said the other ghoul. Only he wasn't a ghoul. When the sunlight struck his face, Rollo was shocked to see that it was none other than Stygius Rex.

"That mount is yours," said the sorcerer, pointing to a skittish gray stallion.

The young troll walked uncertainly toward the horse, and it snorted and backed away. "Why are they wet?" he asked.

"We had to ford the river upstream," slobbered General Drool. On the word "upstream," he spit all over the troll. "Don't ask where. The location of the ford is a secret, and we will keep it that way."

The ghoul caught the horse by the reins and handed them to Rollo. The young troll looked at the strips of leather as if he had no idea what to do with them.

"Don't any trolls know how to ride?" asked Drool.

"No," said Rollo, "they don't give us any horses. They're afraid we'll eat them."

Stygius Rex gave a cackling laugh. "Yes, we haven't treated you trolls very well, have we? With your example, perhaps we can do better. But first we're going on a little scouting expedition."

"Oh, really? Where?" asked Rollo.

"The Great Chasm," answered Stygius Rex. He flicked his finger, and Rollo rose off the ground, his legs kicking in surprise. The sorcerer dropped him into his saddle, still holding the reins. The gray steed stomped for a moment but settled down when the troll stroked his neck.

"Flying you is easy now," said Stygius Rex smugly. "For a few gifted persons, my magic is contagious. In fact, Rollo, you might even be able to fly *alone* someday. Only with my training, of course."

Rollo wanted to ask if they could fly right now, instead of riding these brutish animals. But he nodded and said, "That would be an honor, sir."

The sorcerer took the reins of his own ebony steed and hauled himself into a jewel-encrusted saddle. "Runt tells me that you pointed out Master Krunkle. That was a great help, my lad. It's clear that you are going to be very useful to us."

"I'm trying, sir," answered the troll. "And how is Master Krunkle?"

The wizard gave him a sly smile. "He is also sympathetic to magic." He nudged his horse and took off toward the sun, away from the noisy river.

General Drool jumped onto his fiery black horse and gazed pointedly at the young troll. Foam dripped from the ghoul's rotting nose and slithered down his slack lips. "The master likes you, but remember who's in charge. Him first, me second, you way down on the list."

"Y-Yes, sir!" stammered Rollo. He tried to salute but instead slapped himself with his reins.

General Drool made a croaking sound, and his horse took off in the direction of the sorcerer. Fortunately, Rollo's horse followed without the troll having to do anything. There were stirrups, and after a while, Rollo managed to get his feet into them. After that it was more comfortable sitting in the saddle.

Still, the troll was glad when they stopped to water and rest the horses. He climbed down and tried to straighten up. His rump felt as sore as it had when the snapper took a bite of it.

That all seems so long ago, but it was only a few days, thought Rollo. What were his mother, father, and sister doing? Were they mourning his absence, or were they glad to have more room and more food? They could probably guess where he had gone, because a third of the village was here.

What about Ludicra? Did she even know he was missing? She surely knew Master Krunkle had been trollnapped. Who was teaching the apprentices? Rollo felt oddly nostalgic for the old swamp and his boring life. Every day was the same in Troll Town—not like this, dashing about with the rulers of Bonespittle.

Stygius Rex and General Drool kept to themselves. For a brief period, they studied a map and decided that they knew where they were.

Soon they were back on the move, winding into rugged, mountainous terrain. This land had an ageless, blasted look to it. There were stunted, twisted trees; big, cracked boulders; and gullies filled with shiny black stones. It seemed as if something terrible had happened here, although a long time ago.

What would Ludicra think if she saw him now? wondered Rollo. Would she be impressed? His companions were the most infamous people in Bonespittle. It was an honor to be traveling with them, even if they weren't very good company. Of course, if he didn't make it home alive, the honor wouldn't mean very much.

Stygius Rex and General Drool rode as if they were being chased by crazed elves. The young troll marveled at the endurance of the old sorcerer. More than once, he thought he saw the mage close his eyes and mutter words under his breath. Maybe he was using magic to keep himself going.

As they pounded steadily uphill, briars nicked their horses' legs, and sulfurous smells filled the air. It was not the most pleasant part of Bonespittle; Rollo knew why nobody lived here.

They came upon it suddenly, after climbing the last of a dozen rises. Rollo gasped. The tiny party was dwarfed by the biggest stretch of nothingness he had ever seen. The gash in the earth had to be half-a-league wide, and it seemed endless in both directions. Bottomless, too.

The canyon walls were sheer, as if they had been cut with a sharp axe. He could see the striped patterns of rock and dirt, but only a few mosses and lichen seemed to grow in the Great Chasm. The peculiar smell was coming from somewhere far below.

Just as startling was the difference between the two lands. On their side, the land was blasted and eerie, with hardly a trace of life. The other side boasted a lush forest that was as vast as it was green. The Bonny Woods didn't even seem part of the same planet as their side. He was glad they had come upon this wonder in daylight.

"Horrid sight, isn't it?" asked Stygius Rex with a sneer. "Best get off and tie up our horses. I want to go across while there's still daylight."

Rollo gulped. "Excuse me, Master, you didn't say we were . . . uh, going across."

"You must scout the enemy where the enemy lives," said General Drool. He quickly dismounted and motioned to Rollo to do the same.

"Isn't there someplace where it's not . . . so wide?" asked Rollo as he slid awkwardly off his horse.

"The chasm is the same as this for its whole length," answered Stygius Rex. "It ends in a frigid glacier to the north and a live volcano to the south. For now, there's only one way to cross—to fly."

Rollo laughed nervously. "Yes, sir, then we've got to do it, haven't we? I was just pointing out that it's a long way down. Uh, what's at the bottom?"

"A perpetual stream of boiling lava." The wizened sorcerer gave a weary sigh. "We need to string safety nets all the way across—to protect our workers. But we're worried that the fairies and elves will attack us or destroy the nets."

He gazed into the nothingness. "We just want to see if they have settlements nearby. Maybe there are no elves or fairies in this area, and we won't have to worry. Or maybe we'll put the bridge somewhere else. Ideally, we would like to finish the bridge before they even know about it."

The young troll nodded, because that made sense to him. Still, there were no safety nets over the Great Chasm at the moment. It was a long way to fall just to land in hot lava.

While Drool tied up the horses and Stygius Rex sat on a rock, Rollo tiptoed closer to the Great Chasm. Cautiously, he peered over the edge, and his jutting jaw dropped. He couldn't even see the bottom! He did see some sulfurous mists far below, but they looked like clouds. It felt as if he were staring into the sky—not into the bottom of an abyss.

General Drool stepped beside Rollo and handed him a deadly looking knife with snakes carved into the ebony handle. "Do you know how to use this?"

"To cut ropes and eels," answered the troll uncertainly.

"Necks are exactly the same," said the ghoul with a sly wheeze. "This is a *special* knife. Put it in your belt and guard it well."

Something else to worry about, thought Rollo. He did as he was told.

Behind him, Stygius Rex muttered a few words and threw his hands into the air, and Rollo was *flying!* The troll, the ghoul, and the sorcerer soared over the massive crevice, with the wind pummeling them.

Taking a deep breath, Rollo remembered the things he had told his crew when they were flying over the Rawchill River: *Don't look down! Imagine yourself to be a cloud!*

Luckily, there were many clouds in the sky, and it wasn't hard to imagine being a wisp of fluff caught in the breeze. His heart lifted while his stomach bobbed, and Rollo began to feel more confident.

Cautiously, he lowered his eyes and found himself gazing at the lush forest on the other side. Their destination was like something from a ghoul's nightmare. It was cheery and sunny, with vibrant trees, leafy ferns, and gorgeous waterfalls trickling off the edge.

Rollo knew that a proper troll should loathe such a place, but he couldn't help but be enchanted. The thought of landing there gave a boost to his flight.

He turned his gaze to his companions and saw that he was zooming ahead of them. General Drool appeared calm and fearless; his cape flowed behind him like a wake of black smoke. *Then again,* thought Rollo, *I guess dead people often look calm and fearless.*

Stygius Rex was concentrating, but he took time to nod at the troll, as if saying, "Good job!"

When Rollo turned around, thick trees were rushing straight toward him. "Master! *Help!*" he yelled, but the wind blasted the words back into his face.

The frightened troll soared across the sky like a stone shot from a catapult. With a yell, he crashed into the leafy boughs of the Bonny Woods.

CHAPTER 13
CONTACT

THE CHIRPING, SINGING, AND CAWING OF BIRDS SEEPED INTO Rollo's mind, slowly waking him. These lighthearted sounds were the first thing he noticed, and the second thing was a dull pain in his head. The troll touched a large bump on his forehead and wondered how he had gotten it.

Oh, right, I was flying. Must have run into a tree.

Rollo opened his eyes and gazed up to see green leafy branches all around him. Running into a tree would not be difficult in this place. The growth was so thick that he couldn't see the sky, and it was as dark as twilight in the lush forest. The scent of flowers and fresh dew assaulted his nose, and the pleasant smells made the pain go away a little.

The young troll lay on the forest floor for several minutes, just listening to the birds. In Bonespittle, they had a few fowl, mostly crows and vultures. Here, in the Bonny Woods, he could hear at least ten different birdcalls. And he could see many of the feathered creatures flitting from branch to branch.

There were little birds with sparkling breasts of gold, ruby, and sapphire. There were big birds with colorful crests, long tails, and curved yellow beaks. He watched one that was the color of flames, and the troll thought he had never seen anything so beautiful.

Rollo would have been happy to lie there forever, listening to the birds, but he heard a branch snap. At once, the feathered creatures darted in all directions, screeching in alarm. Rollo quickly saw why. A putrid, bony face leaned over him and dropped a glob of saliva onto his forehead.

"Are you having fun?" asked General Drool in his slurping, wheezing voice.

The troll moved out of the way of the ghoul's drool. "I'm all right now, but it sure hurt when I hit that tree."

"You went too fast," observed General Drool. "No more showing off."

More branches snapped, and Stygius Rex shuffled into view. "It's impossible to walk through this blasted woods!" complained the old sorcerer. He pulled some dewy moss off his black cloak. "Only *butterflies* would want to live here! When we're in charge, we'll get rid of all these stupid trees. This would be a good place for a sludge pile!"

"It is kind of pretty," said Rollo, touching the bump on his head.

"Exactly." Stygius Rex crinkled his face and shivered with disgust. "On your feet, troll. We need to scout this area. Then we make camp and wait until darkness."

Rollo sat up and brushed the leaves off his scraggly fur. Something jabbed him in the stomach, and he touched the scaly handle of the knife in his belt. When he remembered that General Drool had given him the snake knife, he jerked his hand back.

The big troll scrambled to his feet and stretched his arms. All three surveyed the forest but didn't see anything except for towering stands of vegetation.

Sniffing more delicious aromas, Rollo realized that colorful flowers grew everywhere. Vibrant blossoms were all over the ground, and others sprouted from thick vines that entwined the trees like jeweled necklaces. The birds were returning to their roosts, and swarms of insects ebbed through the trees. The Bonny Woods abounded with life.

Stygius Rex turned to Rollo and scowled. "When I am flying with you, you must take some control. I can't do it all. Envision where you want to land, and do it softly. With your antics, you may have given us away."

"Sorry, sir," answered the young troll, bowing his head. He tried not to grin at how well he was doing.

"We must wait for night to move at all," declared General Drool. His oozing eye sockets narrowed. "As much as I hate it, we should camp high in the trees to keep watch. On the ground, we are vulnerable to attack."

Rollo cocked his head thoughtfully. "If the forest is so thick here, maybe the elves and fairies live somewhere else."

Suddenly an arrow sailed past Rollo and stuck firmly in the ghoul's chest. Rollo ducked to the ground, but he kept his eyes on General Drool, who only looked annoyed by the attack. Stygius Rex closed his eyes and slumped to the ground. In desperation and fear, Rollo turned his attention back to General Drool.

The ghoul growled and shook like a dog, causing pieces of rotting flesh to fly in all directions. Ugly green foam oozed from the wound in his chest, and Rollo almost gagged. He wondered if the arrow was poisoned, although it didn't make much difference to General Drool.

The leader of the ghouls ripped the arrow from his foaming chest and tossed it away. Then he drew his long, double-edged sword and went crashing into the woods, chopping everything in his path to bits.

Rollo wanted to charge after him—to help—but he didn't. Another arrow came streaking from the trees, making straight for his head. Before he could even duck, the arrow seemed to strike an invisible wall and glance off, missing him by several feet.

Rollo instantly looked at Stygius Rex, who gave him a slight smile. The troll heard hacking and whacking sounds in the forest. He tried to spot General Drool, but he couldn't. For what seemed like forever, Rollo crouched in fear, but no more arrows came zooming out of the thickets.

In due time, General Drool came shuffling back toward them. "There was only one," reported the ghoul, "and he escaped."

The sorcerer sat up, looking well rested. "Was it a sentry?"

"Perhaps. I never got a good look at him."

Stygius Rex scowled at Rollo. "So much for our quiet arrival. As you suggested, General, we must take to the trees. We don't want to leave any tracks for those fiends to follow."

"Yes, Master," answered the ghoul.

Drool helped the sorcerer to his feet while Rollo looked around nervously. The troll didn't like the idea that someone could be watching them, and that those creatures had bows and arrows.

Rollo thought about the way the arrow had changed course, and he turned to look at the sorcerer. "Excuse me, Master . . . were you protecting us with a spell?"

"Yes, and it was a good thing for you," snapped the old mage. "But I can't keep doing that. We have to use our wits more than my magic." He pointed to a monstrous tree covered with flowering vines. "Start climbing."

From a youth spent in Dismal Swamp, Rollo was experienced at scaling vines. The vines that encircled the massive tree weren't even muddy and thorny like those in the swamp. Still, the feel of the thick strands made the young troll homesick, and he climbed with more fear than joy in his heart.

As Rollo climbed higher, the vines dwindled to mere sprouts, and the boughs dipped under his weight. His knees shaking, Rollo ventured onto a slender branch. Above him sunlight sparkled through holes in the leafy canopy, but it was still far away. The big troll hesitated while swaying back and forth on the flimsy branch.

"Be still down there!" hissed a voice. "We're not alone."

Rollo craned his neck upward to see Stygius Rex high above him, perched among the upper branches. He wanted to ask how he had gotten up there, but he knew the aged mage had his means.

"I'm afraid I'm going to fall," whispered Rollo.

"Don't do it right now," snapped Stygius Rex. "Drool is still down there."

"Doing what?" asked Rollo as he swayed back and forth on the flimsy branch.

"Doing something he does very well . . . playing dead." The old sorcerer rose upward until he was just a speck on the sunlight twinkling through the leaves.

Rollo managed to back up along the narrow branch and retreat to a crux in the branches where he could stand. Finding a sturdy vine and hanging on for dear life, he leaned over and gazed toward the ground. The troll tried to spot General Drool among the leaves, but he got dizzy and had to pull his head back.

When Rollo heard voices, he held his breath. The troll hunkered down to listen more closely, and he heard a branch snap. He gazed upward, trying to spot Stygius Rex at the top of the tree. The sorcerer was holding perfectly still, which meant that the voices and noises were coming from below.

An insect buzzed around Rollo's head, and he brushed it off. He was too busy trying to listen to what was happening beneath him to worry about some big dragonfly. The voices were very clear now, and they were higher pitched than a troll's or a ghoul's voice. They sounded a bit surprised that the intruders had disappeared.

Or maybe they were trying to decide what to do about the decaying body they had found. That would be General Drool in his most effective disguise: himself.

The buzzing returned, and Rollo waved his hand at a huge insect. It had to be a foot long and was brightly colored like a butterfly. However, its wings were a blur of motion, and it moved like a dragonfly. The thing darted behind the tree trunk before Rollo could get a good look at it.

We have big bugs in the swamp, he thought, *but this is ridiculous.*

He heard some leaves rustle, and he looked up to see Stygius Rex creeping down. The cadaverous mage lowered his head through the canopy of leaves and listened intently. Rollo held his breath so as not to make a sound and interfere with the mage's concentration.

"What are you?" asked a lilting voice in his right ear.

Startled, Rollo jumped and banged his head on a branch above him. He stifled a cry, but Stygius Rex still glared at him, his eyes like searing coals. Rollo huddled in the crux of two large branches, gripping the vines for safety. He didn't want to move or get in the sorcerer's way again.

Then a miraculous apparition appeared in front of Rollo, and he had to stifle another cry. It was the insect he had seen before—only it wasn't truly an insect. For one thing, it had a head, arms, and legs, and it seemed to be female.

He rubbed his eyes, thinking he was going crazy from being at such an unnatural height. Then he heard the soft voice again. "What are you?"

Screwing up his courage, Rollo opened his eyes to see the shimmering creature still hovering in front of him. Her wings whirred like the mighty wings of a hummingbird, holding her perfectly still. Her skin was pale and translucent, as were her silky wings.

She cocked her head pertly. "I don't know your kind. What are you?"

"A troll," he whispered. "And trolls shouldn't be in trees, or we imagine things like you."

A whoosh roared in his ears, and the air turned into an oven. The breath was sucked out of his lungs as a blazing ball of fire zoomed past, headed straight down. Flames and embers erupted in its wake, and the air filled with smoke. With a cry, the troll realized that his own fur was on fire, and he patted his singed skin to put it out.

The fireball struck a trunk far below and exploded in a brilliant flash, which shook the mighty tree. Rollo hung on to the vines until the shaking stopped, then he looked in vain for the winged being. She had either escaped or had been burned to a cinder. Or maybe he had imagined her.

His eyes followed the path of smoke and destruction through the smoldering leaves. With all the smoke, he couldn't see anything on the ground, but he could hear screams and shouts. Above him, he heard insane cackling, so he guessed that the fireball had come from their side.

"Good shot, sir!" Rollo managed to shout.

"No, I missed them by a mile," said the sorcerer with a wheezing laugh. "But it's still great fun! By the way, Rollo, I saved you from a fairy that was about to enchant you."

"A fairy? Surely not that pretty insect," answered the troll. "The one who could talk."

Rollo's heavy brow knitted with confusion. It was hard to believe that such a whimsical creature could be the enemy. Just then, the fairy suddenly reappeared in front of him, looking very cross.

She frowned darkly and made a circle with one delicate hand while she pointed the other hand straight at him. Rollo knew he should escape—that he was in grave danger—but he was enchanted by the dainty being in front of him. He was also stuck in a wobbly tree and couldn't move.

"Help!" he muttered, just as a glittering beam shot from her finger into his chest. Rollo winced, expecting to be turned into a pile of beetle dung. Instead, the big troll felt the most awful sensation—a prickly, itchy burning on the bottom of his feet.

With a howl, Rollo took his hands off the vines and madly began to scratch his feet. The more he scratched, the worse it became—but he couldn't ignore the intense itching! For one thing, he couldn't walk or even climb, and he was in real danger of falling out of the tree. "Help!" he bellowed.

Another fireball came streaking out of the upper branches, blowing by Rollo with the hot breath of a furnace. The rush of wind yanked him off his perch, but he caught a vine as he fell. When an explosion shook the tree, Rollo nearly lost his grip, but he hung on to the vine as he dangled over the burning forest.

More than anything, he wanted to scratch his feet, but he had to grip with both hands. "Help!" he cried weakly.

"Maybe that will teach them to leave us alone—not start anything," said Stygius Rex with satisfaction. "Come, lad, let's go. I spotted a bluff not far from here, and I must rest until darkness."

Rollo's stomach fluttered, and he began to float. When he realized he was flying, the young troll felt a sense of relief. He let go of the vine and crashed upward through a wall of thick branches, tumbling into the sparkling sunshine.

A second later, Rollo stopped spinning and straightened out his flight. He tried to follow the dark figure sailing ahead of him. Stygius Rex looked like a dead leaf caught in a hurricane as he soared toward safety.

Rollo could see the ancient bluff rising in the distance. Craggy, barren, uninviting—just the place for visitors from Bonespittle. It looked as if there was no way to scale the cliff by foot, so they should be safe at the top.

He remembered he was supposed to control his own flight, and that the sorcerer's magic was contagious. By concentrating, Rollo found he could increase speed and close the distance between him and Stygius Rex. His feet still itched like mad, and he lifted them to let the cool air flow past.

The troll looked over his shoulder and saw a plume of gray smoke rising from the pristine forest. He felt guilty about that fire, because it was *his* fault they had been seen. Then again, they had been attacked first, without doing anything. Without the sorcerer's protection, Rollo knew he would look like a pincushion by now.

The young troll was so rattled by these events that he just wanted to get to safety. The rugged bluff was looming closer, and he braced himself for a rough landing. When Stygius Rex slowed down, he tried to do the same. By concentrating hard, he found he could control his speed. Both he and the sorcerer landed softly on a narrow ledge.

Rollo slumped against the rock wall, breathing hard, while Stygius Rex studied the area. The sorcerer clucked with delight when he found a small cave. It was really just an indentation in the rock, but there was enough room for the old sorcerer to crawl inside.

Stygius Rex curled into a ball and yawned. "You stay on

guard, Rollo. Cover yourself with bushes or leaves, so they won't see you. Don't disturb me until it's dark."

The young troll looked worriedly at the lush forest that surrounded them. Armies could be hiding in there. Beyond the sea of green was the Great Chasm and the withered brown desert, marking the border of Bonespittle. It looked as if all the life had flowed to one side of the world, and someone had hacked a great cleft to keep it there.

Closer to them, Rollo could see the smoke from the fire coiling into the sky. Then he realized they were missing one member of their party. "What about General Drool?" he asked.

The sorcerer chuckled. "Don't worry about him. He'll find his way to us. Don't wake me up unless there's real danger."

"Yes, sir." Rollo gulped and looked down. It would be hard for anyone to sneak up on them, but that didn't bring him much comfort. Despite the beauty of the Bonny Woods, danger lurked everywhere.

Rollo broke off a few twigs from a nearby bush and tried to camouflage himself. He found that by sitting back from the ledge, he would be unseen to anyone from below. Of course, he couldn't see anyone down there either.

The itching on his feet had lessened to a mild prickling sensation. Still, the young troll kept scratching as he surveyed the vast, gleaming forest. He wondered if he would ever get home to his simple, little swamp.

CHAPTER 14

WALKING AFTER MIDNIGHT

A S DARKNESS DESCENDED OVER THE MIGHTY WOODS, Rollo began to notice spots of light in the distance. *They might be villages,* he realized. He was intrigued by what he had seen so far, but he didn't really want to meet any more locals.

The fire in the woods, which they had started, was down to a few embers and a rope of smoke. Still, a chunk of trees was gone, and he would be glad when true darkness came and he didn't have to see the charred wound in the forest.

For some odd reason, his feet began to itch once more, and he began to scratch. Rollo moved around so much in his scratching that he shed some of his camouflage branches. But it was finally getting dark, so he was getting more relaxed. The troll yawned and heard a lilting voice whisper in his ear, "You are sleepy."

"I can't fall asleep," he muttered, forcing his eyes to open. "If they found me—"

"Are you their servant?" asked the voice.

Now Rollo's eyes sprang wide open. He made out a strange shadow fluttering in front of him. Quickly the troll tried to cover his feet before they got even itchier.

"You . . . g-go away!" he warned the fairy. Clumsily, he drew the knife that General Drool had given him.

"You're from Bonespittle," said the fairy, swooping toward the Great Chasm. A moment later, the whirring shadow shot back in front of him. "I didn't know you could *fly!*"

"Me neither," muttered the troll. He waved the knife around. "I warn you, I know how to use this!"

"I don't think so," she said with a twinkling laugh. "What do you want here?"

Rollo frowned, since that was a logical question. "Just a visit," he said. "Can't we come for a visit without being attacked?"

"Is that all you want?" asked the silky voice. "To talk to us?"

"Well, it would be a start," said Rollo earnestly. He realized that if they could talk the fairies and elves into accepting the bridge, it would avoid a lot of problems.

"That could be arranged . . . maybe," said the fairy. "Have you ever tried to get fairies to agree on anything?"

"No," answered Rollo.

"Don't," she warned him. "My name is Clipper."

"I'm Rollo." The troll sniffed, and his longish ears perked up. "I smell something."

"What?" asked Clipper breathlessly.

"A certain ghoul," he whispered. "Go away!" Rollo waved the knife in the air, and the flitting shadow disappeared.

"She's gone," said a voice, only it wasn't General Drool, as he had expected. He looked back and saw the old sorcerer shaking the leaves off his luxurious cloak.

Rollo recoiled in fear. "I . . . uh, I only talked to her for a moment."

"I heard everything," said the sorcerer with a curl of his lips. "Perhaps you have gained us free passage through this dreadful jungle. Well done. That's why I brought you along, Rollo—to lend our party a touch of innocence."

"Then again," slurred another voice, "he has given away our position."

Rollo whirled to see General Drool standing on the ledge. The ghoul was his usual gruesome self, except that his cloak was all burned and his face was charred. He smelled like rancid meat that had fallen into the fire.

"I found a path," reported the ghoul. "It goes east from here."

"Let's take it," answered Stygius Rex. "I feel much safer now that it's night. Besides, we have an ambassador in our midst."

He slapped Rollo on the back, forcing a nervous smile

from the troll. In response, General Drool made a rude slurping sound.

The ghoul turned and jumped down to a lower ledge, and Rollo dutifully followed. They slid on their rear ends down the rock face—it was so steep, they had to fly a few times. Finally they reached the bottom of the bluff, putting them back into the ominous forest.

Like most residents of Bonespittle, Rollo could see well at night, but he could barely see his own itching feet in this blackness. Even though they were on a path, he kept tripping over bushes and roots. It was slow going until Stygius Rex lit a small, shuttered lantern. He was careful to keep the lamp low, so as to light the path only.

General Drool moved ahead, apparently seeing very well in the dark. The ghoul halted suddenly, and Rollo nearly ran into him. Stygius Rex lifted the lantern, and Rollo saw exactly why the ghoul had stopped.

They faced a strange collection of objects hanging from a trellis erected along the path. There were animal skulls decorated with feathers; small ceremonial bows and arrows; long strands of colorful beads; and embroidered patches. The hodgepodge looked oddly inviting, thought Rollo.

Stygius Rex peered curiously at the artifacts. "These are elf fetishes. They probably tell us which tribe runs this part of the forest."

"This one looks like a map," said Rollo, pointing to one of the odd embroideries.

"So it does." General Drool plucked the piece of embroidery off the trellis and studied it with his empty eye sockets.

"Lead us to the nearest village," ordered Stygius Rex. "I don't think they'll give us any trouble. If they do, I'll burn this wretched place to the ground."

"Yes, Master." General Drool set off at a stiff-legged gait, and Rollo quickly followed the ghoul. He felt the impatient glare of the sorcerer behind him.

After a long walk, the troll declared, "I'm getting hungry." He was hoping the sorcerer would say they could go home to Bonespittle and the delicious meals in the ogre camp.

"Drool has food. Give him a bit of gopher jerky."

"Yes, Master." The ghoul drew some strips of pink meat from his pack and tossed them to Rollo. The troll ate hungrily as they walked.

"Don't you think we know enough about these people?" asked Rollo, wiping his mouth with a furry hand. "They seem to live around here, right next to the chasm. Do you think they'll let us build a bridge?"

"That's what we've come to find out," answered Stygius Rex. "Under the circumstances, I think we're getting along fairly well."

General Drool made a gurgling chuckle. "You mean, they are afraid of you."

"Fear has always worked for me," said the sorcerer with a shrug. "But we are negotiating. They have their ambassador, and we have ours: Rollo."

The ghoul wheezed with disgust and strode off down the path.

"Master," said Rollo hopefully, "does that mean you won't hurt the fairy if she reappears?"

"Not as long as she's helpful," said the sorcerer with a glint in his rheumy eye. "You have been discussing safe passage through this land, and that's fine. However, you are to say nothing about building the bridge. Some of them can fly, some of us can fly—so there's no reason not to be friendly neighbors."

The sorcerer lowered his voice to add, "Rest assured, Rollo, we will not build the bridge here. From maps and questions, perhaps we can learn exactly *where* to build it."

"Yes, sir," answered Rollo with relief. Who was he to question the terrible sorcerer? The young troll told himself not to think too much, like his sister always said he did. The way to survive was to do as he was told, and nothing more.

Seen from a well-worn footpath, by night, the Bonny Woods wasn't so scary. Of course, Rollo couldn't see more than a few feet ahead of him. The birds continued to sing and chatter as they fluttered between the black boughs. Rollo thought he heard different birds from the ones he had heard during the day. The insects joined in, making a shrill noise that penetrated to the troll's spine.

The pungent smell of flowers and rotting loam made his head dizzy, and he forced himself to keep marching. Like the birds, these luscious aromas were more plentiful now than during the day. He couldn't see them, but he imagined the vibrant blossoms all around him.

They walked for a couple of hours before they saw a distant light shimmering between the black tree trunks. Stygius Rex summoned an aura of protection, as he had before, and they pressed cautiously forward.

Moments later, they entered a modest village that featured rows of quaint, cockeyed houses. But no people. In the center of town was a vine-covered gazebo and an old stone well. Between the houses were small vegetable and herb gardens.

The lights proved to be clay pots hanging from tripods. Inside each pot was a candle that cast an eerie orange glow. These modest lights did little to illuminate the village, but Rollo smelled something in the direction of the gazebo.

"Is that what I think it is?" he asked excitedly. The troll led the way toward the circular structure. He climbed the narrow steps and found himself inside the ornate gazebo, with its flowering vines and marble floor. But that's not what made his ears stick straight up.

In the center of the gazebo was a dining table set for dinner. There were three chairs, pitchers of cool drink, and a spread of delicious-looking food.

"They're feeding us!" cried the troll. He attacked the food and began stuffing it into his mouth. Rollo was so busy eating that he hardly noticed when Stygius Rex and General Drool filed in behind him.

"It might be poisoned," said the ghoul.

Rollo instantly spit out a mouthful of food. "Do you really think so?"

Stygius Rex picked up a stalk of celery and sniffed it suspiciously. "Hmmm, disgustingly fresh. Young troll, you go right ahead and eat. I didn't bring a food taster with me, so that's another job you may have."

"Thank you, sir," said Rollo doubtfully. Well, he had already eaten several bites, and he was still alive to eat many more. With both hands, the troll tore into the sumptuous display of food.

"The village is deserted," said General Drool, sniffing the air with a wheezing sound.

"Yes," agreed the sorcerer. "The elves welcome us, leave us a peace offering, but they're afraid to face us. It's rather pathetic."

"I think it's nice," Rollo said through a mouthful of food.

General Drool glared at the young troll, but Stygius Rex laughed. "You're the expert on being nice, Rollo. I just wonder how nice this really is."

"We need more maps," said General Drool as he studied the tapestry he had torn off the trellis. "We need a steady source of information."

"Like a diplomat stationed in the Bonny Woods," said Stygius Rex thoughtfully. "An exchange of diplomats, of course."

"I could do it," Rollo said through cheeks bulging with

food. Any job that would keep the young troll close to this delicious grub would be fine with him. He didn't know the names for any of it, but he had yet to find a bad bite.

"My thoughts exactly," said the sorcerer. "Propose an exchange of ambassadors to your little friend when we see her again. Now you should pick up whatever you can carry, Rollo, because we have to keep moving."

"Yes, Master," said Rollo. The troll began stuffing his pockets and knapsack as quickly as he could stuff his face. When he left the gazebo, General Drool and Stygius Rex were conferring in the middle of the crooked street.

The ghoul sniffed the wind, then he pointed to one of the houses. "Something is alive in there." He strode toward the humble abode with the sorcerer and the troll right behind him.

It was a ramshackle little hut with earthen walls held up by flowering vines. It had wooden slats for a roof. Holes were cut into the sod to make windows, but it still had an earthy appearance that Rollo could appreciate. As if they owned the place, the sorcerer and ghoul opened the front door and walked inside. Both of them had to duck to get under the door frame.

A moment later, General Drool stuck his head out and made a motion for Rollo to stop. "You stand guard," he ordered. "We'll only be a minute."

The troll breathed a sigh of relief. Not only didn't he want to be in those tight quarters with the ghoul and the sorcerer, but he felt it was wrong to enter the house uninvited. He was content to breathe the damp night air and nibble from his new store of food. Rollo kept his eyes open, but nothing moved in the deserted village.

Stygius Rex and General Drool emerged a short time later. The sorcerer carried his lantern, and the ghoul was carrying something, too. It was a tall enclosure with metal bars, and inside of it was a colorful, flashing object.

When Rollo looked closer, he realized it was a cage containing one of the dazzling birds from the forest. This one was mostly scarlet with blue and yellow highlights. Not happy to be in the clutches of the ghoul, the bird flapped its wings helplessly.

"A bird?" asked Rollo. He hoped the ghoul wasn't planning to eat it.

The sorcerer nodded thoughtfully. "Yes, I can do things with birds. Bewitch them . . . make them scout for us . . . see through their eyes. Besides, what's a trip to a new place without bringing home a souvenir?"

"I guess so," answered Rollo. "Does that mean we're going home?"

"Just as soon as we find our way back to the Great Chasm," replied Stygius Rex with a comforting smile. "The general thinks he has found a path that will lead us there."

"I will fill the canteens," said General Drool. He set down the cage, collected their canteens, and walked to the well in the center of town.

That's it? thought Rollo. He knew he should be relieved

that they were finally leaving the dangerous woods, but he felt oddly sad.

"Squawk! Squawk!" said the bird suddenly. "Thieves! Brigands! My master will tan your hides for this. He'll carve your gizzards—he'll twist your toenails!"

Rollo just stared at the talking bird, but Stygius Rex pointed a finger and ordered, "Quiet, you! We'll let you go free if you cooperate with us."

"Well, why didn't you say so?" asked the bird. He promptly ignored them and started preening his long scarlet feathers.

Drool returned with the canteens hanging on his back, and he grabbed the cage. "Is this bird possessed?"

"Of fowl manners," answered the sorcerer with a snort. "But if he behaves, I've offered to free him. So you say you know the way back to the Great Chasm?"

"If the map we have is true," answered Drool. "But it won't be the same place where we crossed."

"No matter," answered Stygius Rex. He lowered his voice to add, "Avoid trouble. I'd like to save my magic to get us across."

"Understood, Master." The ghoul bowed his head, then strode off between two shacks, carrying the birdcage.

Rollo and the sorcerer followed, and they soon found themselves on a different path leading out of the elven village. After a few minutes in darkness, it looked just like the other path. Rollo hoped that General Drool's uncanny sense of direction was still working.

The caged bird began to chirp and sing along with the free birds in the forest. Rollo sped up to walk on Drool's heels so that he could listen to the bird.

"What are you singing about?" asked the troll.

"I'm telling all my friends that I will soon be free! I'll join them in the berry bushes!" the bird twittered happily.

"Why were you imprisoned?"

"Oh, it's a long story," said the bird with a sigh. "To begin with, I'm really a fairy who got enchanted. I made the mistake of falling in love with a snowy egret. Now I'm more of a bird than a fairy, so it's all right. But some people don't like me, and I get in trouble with my mouth. So the rotten elves keep me as a pet."

"You don't like elves?"

"Elves! Ptooie!" The bird spit. "They're always lording it over everyone else, thinking they're better than us. Do you know how that is?"

Yes, thought Rollo.

"They shoot us with arrows, and trap us," complained the bird. "Then they eat us and use our feathers for their silly hats! And you see how useful the elves are when there's trouble? Let a poor bird get stolen right off his perch, they would!"

"They were careless with you," agreed Rollo. A step ahead of him, the ghoul made a rumbling growl, as if to say the conversation was over.

Rollo went back to marching, and it wasn't long before his

feet began to itch. That could only mean one thing: Clipper was nearby.

The troll pretended to stumble, and he dropped to one knee to massage his ankle. Stygius Rex passed by him. "Are you all right, lad?"

"I think it's okay," said the troll. "Go ahead, Master. I'll just have to walk it off."

"Don't fall far behind," warned the sorcerer.

"Yes, sir." He didn't intend to fall far behind. It wasn't necessary in this darkness. Rollo got up and trailed a few paces behind the sorcerer and the ghoul. His eyes darted back and forth, searching for the fairy.

"Didn't you like our food?" asked a voice.

Rollo whirled around to see Clipper hovering above and behind him. "Keep your voice down," he whispered nervously. "I'm not really in charge around here."

"I didn't think so," said Clipper. "Why did you steal that enchanted bird?"

"Remember what I said? I'm not in charge."

"The bird can be dangerous," she warned.

"So can a lot of things around here," answered Rollo. "But don't worry, because we're going home. My master thinks it would be a good idea if your people and our people exchanged ambassadors. For example, you could come live with us, and I could go live in that village . . . with all the good food."

The dainty fairy shook her head, and sparkling dust flew from her curls. "I don't think so. We called many hasty meetings, and I'm sorry to say that nobody in the Bonny Woods wants to have anything to do with you. I thought you would get the hint when you saw the deserted village."

"Don't worry, we're leaving," answered Rollo, feeling defensive over this snub. "Isn't anybody going to see us off?"

She shook her head sadly, and her wings drooped for a moment. "No one is allowed to have any contact with you . . . except for me. This is last time we can meet."

From nowhere, a shadow whipped over the fairy and blotted her out. Rollo stumbled backward, tripped, and fell to the muddy ground. When he rolled back to his knees, he saw General Drool gripping his black cloak, which was flying on its own power over his head.

The poor fairy was trapped in his cloak, zipping this way and that, trying to lose the ghoul. She lifted him a few inches off the ground and rammed him into a tree, then she spun him around in a circle. But the ghoul never let go of his tenacious grip.

Rollo wanted to jump up and help, but he wanted to help Clipper instead of Drool. Unable to do anything, Rollo froze with indecision. When Stygius Rex joined the fight, it was all over for the tiny fairy. They dragged her down into the bushes and subdued her.

Rollo felt sick to his stomach, which was full of all the rich food they had given him.

CHAPTER 15
THE PRISONER

C LIPPER WAS ABOUT A FOOT TALL, ABOUT THE SIZE OF THE
bird she had replaced in the cage, but she seemed a lot
sadder. The fairy looked bruised, defeated, and half-dead as
she lay draped over the perch, trying to stay awake. Her pale
skin was almost white, and the luster had left her eyes. Her
wings hung loosely, and Rollo feared that his brutish comrades had broken them.

The young troll wanted to scold his masters. Clipper
had made friends with *him,* not them. They had no right to
betray that friendship!

But the young troll was afraid to stand up to the
fiendish sorcerer and the gruesome ghoul. Now he knew
why they had stolen what they had from the village: They
wanted the *cage,* not the bird. If Clipper wouldn't agree to

go peacefully to Bonespittle, they would steal her.

Rollo gritted his teeth but tried not to show his anger. If he was going to help Clipper at all, he would have to bide his time. He would have to think hard.

The troll heard a loud caw, and he turned to see the scarlet bird, recently freed from his cage. The enchanted fowl sat on a nearby branch preening himself, pleased with his new station in life.

"Bird," said Stygius Rex, "I have given you your freedom even before you've done anything for me. Can I trust you to fly this path and see if it's clear all the way to the Great Chasm?"

"Anything you say, Master," replied the bird with a bow of his plumed head. "Are you going to make war against the elves?"

"I probably can't avoid it," answered the sorcerer.

"You can count on me to help! I'll muster the birds to your cause. We can fight the fairies, if need be."

Rollo almost mentioned that ogres ate a hundred times more birds than elves did. But he kept silent. Let this foolish popinjay find out for himself. Rollo already knew how horrible it was to help these greedy, selfish conquerors.

Something rustled in the cage, and Rollo turned to see Clipper rise up. She lifted her bruised face and glared at the bird. "Kendo, how can you be such a traitor? You were one of us! Your own foolishness earned you this punishment, and it was too mild. They should have turned you into a dung heap!"

"Can you really do that?" asked Rollo in amazement.

The fairy flashed the troll a look of pure hatred, and her limpid green eyes turned into fire. "There are many things I can do to those who betray me!"

Clipper twisted her arms into a pretzel shape and looked away. A second later, Rollo gave a violent sneeze. He heard another loud noise, and he turned to see Stygius Rex huffing into a black handkerchief. Even General Drool went into a sneezing fit. When the ghoul sneezed, the whole insides of his brain seemed to shoot out his nose.

"Ew!" exclaimed Rollo, turning away. "Achoo!"

"Achoo! Achoo!" echoed Stygius Rex and General Drool.

The bird named Kendo gave a delighted chirp. "Clipper, when it comes to sneezing spells, you are still the best! Don't worry, fellows, you'll get over it in a few hours. I'll go scout ahead." With a whoosh, the colorful bird took off and was gone.

"Cover her up!" ordered Stygius Rex, pointing to the cage. "Ah . . . ah . . . choo!"

At once, Drool threw his cloak over the cage, and all three of them stepped away. But they kept sneezing. Rollo grabbed some leaves to stem the tide from his nose. "I don't know which is worse—this, or the itchy foot. Achoo!"

Stygius Rex sat on the ground for a few minutes and

concentrated. First his sneezing stopped, then Rollo and Drool were able to regain control of their noses. General Drool helped the aged mage to his feet.

"I've contained her," said the sorcerer. "She'll be too weak to use any of her magic. No talking to her, Rollo, until we get home."

"Yes, sir," answered the troll glumly.

"Now let's get moving."

General Drool picked up the birdcage and led the way, with Rollo and Stygius Rex following close behind. They marched along the path with more haste than before. Once it was known that they had captured a fairy, no doubt the locals would come storming after them. Rollo found it hard to believe that they would just allow Clipper to be fairy-napped without a fight.

Then again, Stygius Rex had stolen a few thousand trolls from Troll Town and no one tried to stop him. *He won't be happy until he enslaves all of us,* thought Rollo. *All the evil in Bonespittle comes from this one creature, and I'm helping him!*

I'm on the wrong side.

The young troll thought about running away, just dashing into the dark woods. But he knew he would fall into a bog, a trap, or a hail of arrows. Even if he got away, that wouldn't save Clipper, and he had to save the beautiful fairy before he saved himself.

"Rollo!" said a sharp voice, making him jump.

The troll turned around, fearful that the sorcerer had somehow read his mind. "Yes, Master?"

"You look like you're nightdreaming. Stay awake."

"Yes, sir." The troll gulped and skipped ahead. He would rather walk close to the ghoul, he decided.

It seemed as if they marched through darkness for hours. The deeper they went into the shadowy woods, the quieter it became. *Where are the birds?* wondered Rollo. It was so dark, the troll worried that he would step off the path right into the Great Chasm. He longed to see daylight.

General Drool plowed ahead, the cage swinging easily from his hand. Rollo kept close watch on his bobbing head to make sure the ghoul didn't plunge into the chasm.

The troll tripped and almost fell down. He was forced to back up and keep his feet in the puddle of light cast by the wizard's lantern. In the distance, Rollo could hear a fluttering sound that grew louder with every second.

"They're right on my tail!" screeched a voice. The red bird soared past Rollo's nose, and an arrow was chasing him.

"Ugh! Urgh!" muttered General Drool ahead of him. The ghoul turned around to show two arrows sticking out of his chest. "We are under attack."

In the next instant, a figure leaped into the path ahead of them. It was a lithe creature about five feet tall, with reddish hair and beard.

"An elf!" growled General Drool.

The slender being drew his bow and cocked an arrow

in the notch. The general set down the cage and reached for his sword.

"Duck!" howled a voice. When Rollo saw the ghoul drop like a sack of dirty clothes, he dove to the ground. That was smart, because a roaring, searing fireball whooshed over his head. Like a comet, it swerved down the path into the woods, missing the elf by ten feet. But the effect was so startling that the archer dove out of the way.

Then came the explosion, accompanied by flames, smoke, flying embers, shouts, and chaos. Rollo felt someone grab him by the collar, and he knew it was Stygius Rex. With surprising strength, the old sorcerer pulled him to his feet. General Drool sheathed his sword and grabbed the birdcage while Stygius Rex closed his eyes and started muttering.

As arrows, smoke, and burning embers flew all around them, the three began to rise into the air. Rollo held the sorcerer's arm for support, because he was already crashing through branches. Putting guilt and fear out of his mind, he thought only about flying higher and higher.

The troll rose through the trees like a bubble in the swamp water. Branches kept whipping him in the face, but he fought them off. At last, the troll broke through the tree-tops into a starlit sky. By the full moon, there was finally enough light to look around.

To Rollo's great relief, he saw they were close to the Great Chasm. Even at night, the gaping gorge was the biggest, ugliest landmark in the world. The fissure yawned across the land, separating good from evil, bountiful from stingy. *It* does *have a purpose,* thought Rollo.

The troll tried to steer himself toward the chasm, and he found himself gaining on it. Stygius Rex and General Drool were right behind him, but so was something else. It sounded like a swarm of insects—a giant, buzzing swarm of insects.

Rollo looked over his shoulder and saw a sea of dragonflies silhouetted against the moon. Only they weren't dragonflies, or anything else he had ever seen in such number. They had to be fairies! *Thousands of them!* With their whirring wings, they were bearing down on the invaders like a flock of vultures.

"They're right on top of us!" shouted Rollo.

"Keep flying!" ordered Stygius Rex. "I must land to do battle." The sorcerer alighted among the treetops, and Rollo was afraid to see what would happen next.

"Come!" shouted General Drool as he soared past Rollo. He waved the shrouded birdcage over his head.

Rollo gulped and kept flying toward the chasm, but he glanced back over his shoulder. The forest beneath them was dark and eerily quiet.

Then a fireball erupted from the trees, arced across the moon, and smashed into the flock of fairies. There were so many of them, it couldn't miss. With shrill cries and screams, the fairies scattered throughout the starlit sky. The fireball dropped toward the forest and finally exploded in a shower of sparks.

The fairies regrouped, becoming a dark cloud that dove straight into the trees. Rollo wondered if they were attacking Stygius Rex. In answer, the whole forest erupted in a kaleidoscope of blinding light—like a flash of lightning. Rollo quickly turned his head, but he was still blinded for a few seconds.

"Up to his old tricks," said General Drool.

They flew closer to the ravine, and Rollo felt as if he were sailing on a breeze. When they left the land and forest behind them, he tried not to look down. Crossing the chasm was easier at night, he decided, because there was nothing to see but the faint glow of lava below them.

They soared over the Great Chasm. Rollo was doing fine, but the ghoul began to drop in altitude. The troll descended to stay level with the general, but he was more concerned about Clipper. If he dropped that cage, the fairy would be helpless. Trying not to worry, Rollo kept flying until he could see the barren wastes of Bonespittle.

Home! At the thought of Troll Town, Rollo sped up just as General Drool began to drop farther behind.

"Halt!" called the ghoul. "The master is in trouble! Come back and get the prisoner—"

There was no way Rollo could halt—that would be certain death. But he thought he could swing around and save Clipper. Getting that cage from Drool's hand was exactly what he wanted to do.

"I'm coming!" he promised, but he didn't really know if

he could reverse course. By sheer will, Rollo managed to turn slowly and bank toward the helpless ghoul.

By the time he got there, Drool was hanging in midair. He looked like one of those ogres who was about to drop into the river, but there was no fear in his empty eyes. He held out the cage as Rollo swerved by.

"Guard her well," warned the ghoul. With those words, General Drool dropped out of the sky. With a flapping sound, he plummeted into the dark depths of the abyss.

Rollo was shaken to see a second comrade vanish so suddenly, and he was afraid he would do the same. With all his concentration he kept himself flying toward the edge. He thought briefly about going back to the Bonny Woods, but he was much closer to the Bonespittle side.

To his surprise, the cage felt very light in his hand. He couldn't see the injured fairy because of Drool's cape, and he hoped she was all right.

With huge relief, the troll bounded onto the stark cliffs of Bonespittle. He carefully set the cage on the dry ground, then collapsed beside it. A million thoughts were going through his mind, whirring as fast as the fairies' wings. Was General Drool dead? Would a fall like that kill a ghoul?

More importantly, was Stygius Rex dead?

Rollo looked back to the other side of the chasm and couldn't see anything amiss. There was smoke and fire in the Bonny Woods, but that was to be expected. Rollo was alive, and he was temporarily free of them! Only he wasn't alone.

With trembling fingers, Rollo removed the cloak from the birdcage. He gasped when he saw the poor fairy lying motionless on the bottom. Instantly Rollo snapped the lock, breaking it, then he reached inside the cage. Very carefully, he picked up the fragile prisoner, who felt like a bird with silky feathers.

He didn't touch Clipper's wings, for fear they were broken. They hung limply at her side. To his great relief Rollo could feel her steady breathing in the palm of his hands. Clipper was just asleep, or so it seemed. Rollo suddenly remembered that the sorcerer had cast a spell to keep her quiet. So maybe she would be all right.

Rollo carefully put the fairy back into the cage, then he wrapped Drool's cape over it. It was too much to hope that both Stygius Rex and General Drool were dead. They would expect him to wait by the horses . . . or go back to the big camp at the Rawchill River.

But Rollo wanted to go home, back to Troll Town. If he could just get to the horses before they did, he could really put some distance between them.

Then I'll be a fugitive, the young troll realized. *All the forces of Bonespittle will be sent to chase me down.*

He looked at the cage and realized that he couldn't return the helpless fairy to Stygius Rex. He had to protect her. If the residents of Bonespittle could just see Clipper, they would know they had been fed lies all these years. Not just about the Bonny Woods, but about *everything.* He would

153

take Clipper to Dismal Swamp and let the trolls meet her!

Rollo scanned the horizon on the other side of the chasm, looking for the bluff where they had camped. Once he found it outlined against the stars, he knew which way to go. He picked up the cage and ran along the edge of the chasm, keeping low.

After a while, he could smell the horses in the distance, right where they had been left. When he reached the beasts, he hung the cage from one of them and tied the others behind him. Rollo didn't want to leave any mounts for the sorcerer. Speaking soothing words to his horse, Rollo took the reins and climbed aboard.

As he rode off, the young troll shivered at what he had just done. He had made an enemy of the absolute ruler of Bonespittle—the ruthless sorcerer, Stygius Rex.

CHAPTER 16

ON THE RUN

U NDER THE MEAGER SHADE OF A MISSHAPEN TREE, ROLLO stopped to rest and water the horses. Even though he had been riding all three, switching from one to another, they were spent. Part of the problem was that it was mid-morning and still hot in the high desert. He could see more trees in the distance, but they were many leagues away. Rollo wanted to keep riding, but wasn't sure the horses could take it.

Without the presence of Stygius Rex and General Drool, they were docile animals, very friendly. The steeds were happy to stay in a herd and let the troll lead them home. But he wasn't sure what he would do with them once they got to the Rawchill River.

Rollo was riding wide across the desolate plain to avoid

the big work camp. So he wasn't sure when he would reach the river. Should he camp here, he wondered, and wait until dark? Or should he ride on while it was sunny and there was no one around?

The troll turned to look at the cage on the second horse. He hadn't checked on Clipper for a while, and he hoped the ride hadn't been too bumpy for her. He carefully untied the cage and set it on the ground under the shade. Then he peeled off Drool's black cape.

The poor fairy was still lying unconscious on the bottom. Rollo opened the cage, reached inside, and gently took her limp body in his hand. As soon as he drew her out of the cage, though, the tiny being turned into a whirlwind. She stabbed his palm with something sharp, and the troll cried out and dropped her.

Clipper could have easily taken off into the sky, and she tried to fly. She flapped forcefully with her right wing, but her left wing hung useless. The fairy spiraled in the air for a while and finally landed with a plop on the ground. One of the horses whinnied and stomped nervously.

Rollo frowned at the cut on his hand and the jagged piece of metal sticking out. It was part of the cage. "Why did you cut me?" he asked angrily. "That's the thanks I get for saving your *life?*"

Looking defeated and embarrassed, the fairy lifted herself onto her elbows. "Are you saving me, or are you obeying the orders of Stygius Rex?"

"As of now, I'm a fugitive," grumbled Rollo. "All because of you, my life is completely messed up. I should just leave you here."

"Where are we?" asked the fairy with weariness in her voice. She rose to her feet and looked around at the forsaken desert; there were tears in her jewel-green eyes.

"Bonespittle," answered Rollo. "The *ugly* part of Bonespittle."

"If you really want to help me, why don't you take me back to the Bonny Woods?" Clipper rubbed her nose and stared indignantly at the troll. "They could fix my broken wing."

"I thought about that," muttered Rollo, ducking his head. "But we were so close to this side of the chasm. Plus, I can't fly without help from Stygius Rex, and he was . . . somewhere behind us."

"Burning down the woods?"

"Probably." Rollo was tired of being made to feel guilty. "Look, he stole *me* from my home too! He made me go across the chasm because his flying spell works on me. I'm in big trouble because of this. I've given up everything!"

The troll sniffed with self-pity. "It wasn't a great life, or a very long life. But I really wasn't ready throw it away yet. Now there's no chance to marry Ludicra. So quit complaining, or I'll let them catch us!"

Rollo stomped toward the horses, his feelings hurt. His hand also hurt, and he looked for something in the saddlebags to use as a bandage.

"Rollo," said a lilting voice. "I'm sorry. I should have trusted my first impression of you. I thought you were nice, but your traveling companions were very rude."

"How would you like to have them around all the time?" asked Rollo. Then he sighed. "Well, maybe we got lucky, and that flock of fairies got rid of them."

"We attacked you?"

"You sure did!" Rollo told her all about their dramatic escape over the chasm. He told her how Stygius Rex got left behind, and General Drool got left below. "I've been running ever since," concluded the troll.

"Where are we going?" asked Clipper.

"To my home, Dismal Swamp. We've been told all kind of crazy things about fairies and elves, and I want them to see you. They've got to know you aren't monsters."

"We heard terrible things about you, too," said Clipper with a frown. "Only they all turned out to be true."

"You haven't met all of us," said the troll quickly. "You met the *worst* two of us. We must all look ugly to you, but it's hard to say who's good and who's bad. You think the elves are good, but the birds sure don't."

"That's true," said Clipper with a thoughtful nod. "Rollo, you're very wise for someone so young."

"After what I just did, I'm not so sure of that." He took a handkerchief from the saddlebag and wrapped it around his hand. Clumsily he tied a knot. "And how old are you?"

"Only a few hundred years," she said sweetly. "We live a long time."

Rollo lowered his head. "I'm sorry, Clipper. I know you

didn't want to be the ambassador to Bonespittle, but you got the job anyway."

"Do you have healers?" she asked. "People who can fix my wing? And your hand?"

"We have people who can fix anything," promised the troll. "So you'll come home with me?"

"Yes, but I don't want to ride in that cage anymore." The fairy pointed toward the horse. "Could I ride in those bags on your mount?"

"The saddlebags? Sure," answered Rollo. Carefully, he picked up his new friend and tucked her into the leather pack. "Are you okay in there?"

She popped her petite head out of the bag. "I could use a little water."

"Got plenty of that." Rollo grabbed a canteen and filled up the cap, which he handed to her.

Clipper drank thirstily and wiped her mouth on her delicate arm. "Thank you, Rollo, I'll be okay now. So what are you going to do about him?"

"Do about whom?" asked Rollo innocently.

"You know who. Stygius Rex."

"Um, I . . . I haven't really thought about it." Rollo roped up the horses and the birdcage, not wanting to leave it behind. Then he climbed into his saddle with more grace than before.

"You had better think about it," said the fairy. "We chased him out of the Bonny Woods, and you should chase him out of Bonespittle, too."

Rollo laughed nervously. "Uh, *me?*"

"You know that somebody has to do it," insisted the fairy. "The fey folk have known that something like this was going to happen. We've had dreams and visions . . . plus all the signs were there. That's why the elves have kept so many sentries near the Great Chasm. However, we weren't expecting flying trolls."

"There won't be any flying trolls if we get rid of Stygius Rex," said Rollo sadly.

"Nonsense!" squeaked the voice behind him. "I've seen you, and you fly just fine! I bet you could fly without his help."

"I don't want to try," grumbled the troll. "Come on." He gently kicked his horse, and the caravan trod sluggishly into the morning sun.

Clouds and fog enveloped them about midday, and they were relieved to be out of the heat. Rollo, Clipper, and the horses smelled the river before they saw it. The horses wanted to hurry, but Rollo led them slowly as he looked for signs of the work camp. By the time they got to the river, they had seen nothing but a few horse tracks on the ground. Patrols, he figured.

Rollo noticed that the tracks went upriver, away from the camp, and he decided to follow them. Perhaps the ghouls knew the place to ford the river, and they were headed there. To follow the tracks, he had to dismount and lead the horses.

From the saddlebag came a delicate yawn. "Why don't we fly over right here?" asked Clipper. "It doesn't look very wide. If I had both my wings—"

"Well, you don't," answered Rollo. "And my flying days are over. We'll find a shallow place to walk across with the horses."

Clipper looked doubtfully at the roiling, frigid water. "Walk?"

"Yes, there are places to cross!" said Rollo stubbornly. "I just don't know where they are."

"We'd better find one soon," suggested Clipper, "because I hear hoofbeats behind us."

"What?" The troll stopped in his tracks to listen, and his pointy ears shot up. He did hear faint hooves, but it was hard to tell how close they were over the sound of rushing water.

"We'll have to cross here," he declared. "Right now."

"Why?" asked Clipper. "Maybe these aren't the villains. Maybe these are some of those *good* folks you mentioned."

"I'm afraid the good folks do not have horses . . . not in Bonespittle." Rollo leaped back onto his mount and guided the beast into the rushing water. The animals thought they were just getting a drink, and he let them drink for a few seconds. Then he nudged them forward.

Rollo got about fifty feet into the river when he realized he had made an awful mistake. For one thing, the Rawchill lived up to its name: It was painfully cold. He was riding the biggest horse, General Drool's black steed, but the poor beast got swamped. Rollo tried to turn and start back, but the horse lost his footing and got caught in the strong current.

The troll instantly untied the rope for the other two horses, letting them go free. They were closer to shore and had a chance to escape. Then he heard a scream over the roaring water, and he saw the saddlebags floating away. As the bags bobbed under, Clipper waved her arms helplessly.

With a lunge, Rollo caught the bags, but he fell off his horse. Now they were loose in the frenzied rapids. The troll struggled to swim, but it was no use in the massive current. They weren't far from shore, but it might as well have been a million miles.

Rollo tried to hold the saddlebags high, but he was gasping for breath every time he went under. Something kicked him on the arm, and he looked up to see Clipper hanging from the drenched saddlebags.

"Now!" she screamed. "Take off!"

When his teeth began to chatter, Rollo decided she was right. If he could fly, this was the time to do it. Rollo concentrated and remembered the night he had sailed across this same river. He felt the sensation of soaring over the Great Chasm—not once but twice! With a thrill, the troll recalled the way the air had ruffled his fur during that flight. The sky was his home as much as the swamp.

These pleasant memories cut down some of the chill, but he was still freezing. Rollo almost decided it wasn't working when he forced his eyes open. With amazement, he saw himself skimming over the top of the waves. *I'm flying!* Even without the mage's help, he could do it. The magic had stuck to him!

Rollo didn't have time to savor his feat. The fog was as thick as sleet, and Clipper hung to his extended arm. The shivering fairy gave him a grateful smile, and Rollo cradled her to his chest. He looked back but couldn't see the horses in the thick fog. Rollo was sure at least two of them had made it back to the bank. Drool's big black horse was a strong beast and could probably swim, he told himself.

When they landed on the homeward side of the river, Rollo collapsed onto the ground, shivering. Clipper pinched his arm and breathed, "That was awesome flying, Rollo . . . and a good time to give it a try."

Still, the young troll was glum. "Yeah, thanks."

"What's the matter with you?"

Rollo sat up and looked around at the dreary wasteland. "This is what the rest of my life is going to be like," he muttered. "Running from hoofbeats, ducking from shadows . . . hiding under bridges."

"Until you get rid of Stygius Rex," said Clipper.

"Right." The troll rolled his eyes and rose to his feet. They had lost their saddlebags, saddles, horses, food, and water, and now they were on foot. "Want to sit on my shoulder?" he asked.

"Sounds good," Clipper answered cheerfully.

The troll picked up the soggy fairy and gently shook the water off her. Then he placed her on his shoulder, and she hung on to his dangling earlobe. With the mud squishing between his toes, Rollo headed away from the Rawchill River and toward home.

"That is definitely General Drool's horse," said Captain Chomp, pointing at the drenched, frightened animal. He stood on the distant bank of the Rawchill River along with a detachment of ogres on horseback.

Standing atop a wagon was the little gnome, who nodded thoughtfully. "Yes, that's his horse," said Runt. "But what happened to General Drool? And what happened to Stygius Rex and Rollo?"

"'Tis a mystery," admitted Chomp. "But we'll double the patrols and keep looking for them."

"Yes, yes! You'd better do that!" ordered Runt nervously. He didn't like being in charge, but with the master and General Drool gone, he had to be. "Use as many ogres as you need. Don't rest until you find them!"

"Excuse me," said Lieutenant Weevil. "This horse doesn't mean they were here. They probably left their mounts at the Great Chasm, and maybe the horses ran away before they got back."

"That's right!" exclaimed Runt. "Good thinking, Weevil. Captain Chomp, take your ogres and go to the Great Chasm. Search everywhere between here and there."

"Yes, sir," said the big ogre with resignation. He sniffed along the ground. "Hey, we've got some tracks to follow. We'll find them. All right, everyone, mount up!"

CHAPTER 17
HOME, DISMAL HOME

D AYLIGHT WAS FADING BY THE TIME ROLLO REACHED Troll Town. He wrapped Clipper up in his shirt and carried her like a bundle in case he ran into anyone. It lifted the troll's spirits to scamper across the old bridges, but the village was oddly quiet. This close to twilight, the early risers should be setting up their stands or digging for grubs. Why was Troll Town so quiet?

Nestled in his arms, Clipper poked her head above the top of the bundle. The fairy looked around, then wrinkled her pert nose. "So this is the *beautiful* part of Bonespittle?"

"This is where the trolls live," whispered Rollo. "I've heard that Fungus Meadows is beautiful, but I've never seen it. We're not into beauty, we're into . . . bridges."

"Then it's quite delightful," agreed Clipper.

"It should be busier than this," said Rollo worriedly. "There's something wrong, I think. But we're almost home. Keep your head down."

"There's no one to see us," she protested.

"Trolls can be watching from under the bridges," whispered Rollo. "Trust me on this."

"Okay." The injured fairy burrowed back into the bundle of rags.

Rollo moved furtively along the deserted bridges, listening to the mud ooze and suck in the surrounding bog. Even the swamp monsters seemed to be asleep on this dawn of a new night.

With great relief, Rollo reached the mound where his family lived, and he slid down the greasy old roots. He scampered over the gnarled stoop and tried the door—only to find it locked. Cautiously, he knocked on the door. He had to bang repeatedly before he got a response.

"Go away!" came a tremulous voice. It sounded like no one he knew.

"It's me! Rollo!" he blurted. "I *live* here!"

"No, no, Rollo's at the work camp!" insisted the squeaky voice. "We're too sick from no food . . . nobody in here can work."

"Crawfleece!" shrieked Rollo with amazement. "Please, sister, open the door!"

"How do I know that's really you?"

"It was *you* who wanted me to skim the Hole the other day, which got me in trouble with the ogres. That wasn't the story you told our parents."

"Lucky guess."

The young troll fidgeted nervously while the clicks and clacks of countless bolts and locks sounded. He didn't remember their having that many locks on the door. When he saw his sister in the dim light, all of their squabbles were forgotten, and they hugged each other warmly.

"How did you get away?" called a voice from inside. "Did anyone else get out of the camp?"

"Mother!" Bulling past his sister, the young troll ducked into the hovel. He found his strapping mother in the shadows cast by a single candle, and he hugged her fiercely. Vulgalia didn't feel as bulky as she had when he'd left—her fur just hung on her.

"Have you brought us something to eat?" shrieked Crawfleece, grabbing the bundle from his arms.

She rushed to the cold fire pit, set the morsel on the logs, and tore off the rags. Clipper spilled out into the ashes, then she leaped to her feet, looking furious.

Crawfleece clapped her hands. "Oooh, good! You brought us a great big . . . what is it? A flying fish?"

"You'll not eat me . . . you brutes!" Clipper shook the ashes off her wings, then she started twisting her arms together.

"No, no!" shouted Rollo, rushing to the fire pit. "This is my friend, Clipper!" He pushed his sister back, then turned his attention to the fairy. To his relief, she had stopped twisting her arms to summon a spell.

"They're not themselves," he explained to his guest. "Something terrible has happened here."

"We don't have any food," said his mother accusingly, "and you bring us *another* mouth to feed? Although it is a very tiny mouth."

"What is she?" asked Crawfleece, peering curiously at the fey creature.

"A fairy," answered Rollo. "From the other side of the Great Chasm."

The two female trolls blinked in surprise. "That can't be a *fairy,*" scoffed Crawfleece, sounding like her old self again. "They're big and ferocious. Someone is ribbing you, little brother."

Clipper laughed with amusement. When she saw the serious expression on Rollo's face, she grew somber again.

"Look, mine is a long story," said the young troll. "Yours is probably shorter. What has happened here?"

His mother sniffed back tears and sat dejectedly on the earthen floor. "The first night, we heard from witnesses that you had been taken by the ghouls and ogres. But you get along with everyone—we figured you would survive."

She smiled and patted him on the knee. "I'm glad you did. After that, the next couple of nights were normal . . . or as normal as they could be with so many villagers missing. But on the third night, they came for all the food. And I mean *all* the food. They said they needed it to feed the bridge workers."

"More like an army," muttered Crawfleece.

Vulgalia's voice caught, and she sniffed back tears. "Somehow the ghouls found out they had missed your father the first time around. They came and got him two nights ago."

"I must have just missed him in camp," said Rollo angrily, slamming his fist into his palm.

Vulgalia looked with concern at her daughter. "I've been afraid they would come for Crawfleece too. We've all been so afraid . . . Troll Town has dried up like a swamp in a drought."

"Everyone is afraid to leave their homes," said his sister glumly. "But we have to leave, because we have no food. I joined up with some youths who have hidden out, and we want to fight the ghouls. But we don't know where to begin! I don't want to stay here, where they can find us, but Mother refuses to leave this old hovel."

"We worked hard for this hovel!" protested his mom. "It doesn't leak much, the nearby bridges are in good condition, and there are usually grubs in the mud."

"But not anymore," muttered his sister. Crawfleece looked hungrily at the fairy and smacked her lips.

The tiny being stared up at his sister. "Listen to your brother!" she squeaked indignantly. "Rollo has become quite important in your society. When I met him, he was traveling in the Bonny Woods with Stygius Rex and General Drool."

"What?" asked Vulgalia, casting a fearful eye at the portrait of Stygius Rex hanging on the wall. "You *met* them?"

"He was their companion," answered Clipper. "Just the three of them—Rollo, the sorcerer, and the dead man—all very chummy."

His mother looked as if she would faint. "Maybe you had better tell us your story now, son."

Rollo was about to begin when his sister jumped up and locked the door, with much clicking and clacking of bolts. "You can't be too careful," she explained. "We should keep our voices down too."

"Right," answered Rollo, wondering if he should have come here at all. This wasn't the safest place for two fugitives on the run.

"What!" screeched Crawfleece, banging her brother on the head. "You had *horses,* and you didn't bring one home for *dinner?*"

"We lost them when we crossed the river," snapped Clipper, rising to Rollo's defense. "The current was fierce . . . your brother had to fly to get us across that river."

Crawfleece blinked at the fairy. "You mean he had to swim really fast."

"No, I mean he had to lift off the ground and *fly* . . . all by himself."

Rollo's mother was alarmed. "Is that true, son?"

The troll shrugged his beefy shoulders. "I guess so. The first time I flew, it was all because of Stygius Rex and his magic. But he said his magic was contagious for some people. I thought I needed the mage to fly, but"—Rollo glanced gratefully at the smiling fairy—"Clipper told me I could do it, and I could."

Suddenly they heard hoofbeats on the bridge above them, and everyone froze. Crawfleece instantly grabbed the candle and prepared to blow it out. But the hoofbeats were not many, and they continued on. Still, no one breathed until it was totally quiet above them.

"You can't stay here," said his mother sadly. "This will be the first place they come looking for you."

"I guess so," muttered Rollo. "Crawfleece, where are your friends, the ones who are hiding from the patrols?"

"Some stay under the bridges, but most are in the Forgotten Forest," answered his sister.

"A forest?" asked Clipper, her face brightening.

"Yes," answered Rollo, "that would probably be the best place for us. How can I find them?"

"I know their hiding places," she answered proudly. "They go to the Hole for water."

"Then we've got to go there too." Rollo gently picked up Clipper and looked around the hovel for his old knapsack. When he found it, he was glad to see that Clipper fit perfectly in the shoulder bag.

"I'll never see you again!" wailed his mother tearfully. "Just like your father!" She began to sob fitfully, and Rollo took the once-stocky troll in his arms.

"Don't worry about me or Father," he said. "Believe me when I say that Father has never eaten better in his life. As for me, I can *fly!* I will always escape them."

"Yes, my little leechcake," said his mother, patting him sweetly on the cheek. "And so important you are—first you're the companion of the great sorcerer, then you rebel against him." That thought made her burst into tears again.

"Maybe he's dead," said Crawfleece helpfully. She moved toward the door, unlocked it, and opened it a crack. "Come on, Rollo, it's dark now—this is a good time to go. I'll scout ahead for you."

While Crawfleece scampered up to the bridge, Rollo gave his mother another warm hug. Hearing a whistle from his sister, he hefted the bag containing Clipper and scurried into the darkness.

When Rollo caught up with Crawfleece beneath the bridge, he asked her, "How is Ludicra?"

"I don't know," she whispered. "I've heard nothing about her, so I guess she's still hiding. Are you still mooning over her?"

"Just worried," answered the young troll. "I'm worried about everyone."

*　　　*　　　*

Rollo never thought he would be glad to see the Forgotten Forest, especially at night. But the stand of misshapen trees, thorny thickets, and dense moss was like an oasis in the swamp. Finally he could drop to the ground and rest, while he let Clipper out of the bag to take a stretch.

When she looked around, the fairy's mood immediately brightened. Although this creepy grove bore little resemblance to her lush woods, she said she felt at home. Clipper asked Rollo to place her in a tree a few feet off the ground, where she made herself a nest out of dried leaves and moss.

Crawfleece left them to find her compatriots in the woods. Rollo wished that everything could go back to the way it was . . . to the day before Stygius Rex came to their village. But how could it?

With a delicate yawn, the fairy lay down in her nest to get some sleep. "Good night, Rollo."

"You sleep at night?" he asked in amazement.

"We often play in the early evening and go to bed after midnight," answered Clipper. "That gives us all day to fly around."

Rollo bowed his head sheepishly. "I'm sorry we didn't have time to find someone to fix your wing."

"That's all right," she answered sweetly. "Now that I've seen how trolls are treated in Bonespittle, I feel more sorry for *you* than for me. Our own healers will fix my wing. I have faith in you, Rollo, that you will take me to *my* home when we're done here."

"I promise," said the troll. "I will get you home."

"Now you have to sleep," Clipper insisted. "I know your stomach is growling, but you haven't slept in a long time. You need your energy for tomorrow."

"You're right," he said with a yawn. Maybe a few winks wouldn't hurt, even if it was still night. The big troll curled up on a bed of leaves and ferns.

As soon as he shut his eyes, he was asleep.

CHAPTER 18
LATE IN THE DAY

GOOD-NATURED LAUGHTER ROUSED ROLLO FROM A DEEP sleep, and he thought he was still dreaming. When he heard some sneezes, he figured he had better wake up. That could only mean that Clipper was in trouble and defending herself.

Rollo rose to his knees and had to shield his eyes from the sunlight. The Forgotten Forest wasn't like the Bonny Woods—plenty of sunshine filtered through the withered weeds and bedraggled boughs. This light had the golden glow of late afternoon, meaning he had slept too long.

The troll jumped to his feet, thinking he would have to save Clipper, because she had used her sneezing spell. Then he heard laughter, and he followed the sound through the underbrush to a gaggle of trolls.

In the center of this bunch he found Clipper, dancing and pirouetting like a dust devil. Occasionally she made a wild spin, and someone in the audience would start sneezing or scratching their feet. When this happened, the other trolls howled with laughter, Crawfleece loudest of all.

Rollo was surprised to see that these refugees were young and old, male and female, with several children mixed in. There were at least forty of them. *These people are like me,* he realized. *They've given up their homes to defy Stygius Rex.*

"Good morning, Rollo!" Clipper called with a wave. She finished her act to much applause and ran toward him, holding her injured wing with the opposite hand.

She beamed up at him. "I told them all about your bravery at the Great Chasm. Would you believe that elves and trolls have the same taste in humor?"

"I would," the troll answered with a confused smile. He looked at the audience, whose smiles were fading as they considered the gloomy wilderness all around them. The only good hiding places were the thorny thickets and shrubs, plus the bogs, if they didn't have monsters in them.

Rollo heaved his brawny shoulders. "Is there anybody in charge here?"

"No one," answered a raspy voice. "But I know *who* should be in charge." From the back of the gathered throng, a frail figure limped forward. He was using a crutch on one arm, and a young female held his other arm. The old troll was so beaten and feeble that Rollo didn't recognize him at first.

When he did, he gasped. "Master Krunkle!"

Rollo rushed forward to grasp his old teacher by the shoulders. He had last seen him under the curse of Stygius Rex, looking as dead as a ghoul. "How did you get away? Are you all right, sir?"

Krunkle nodded and motioned to Rollo to let him sit in the dirt. They both sank down to the ground, and everyone else hunkered around them. "Keep the guards alert," ordered Krunkle.

"Yes, sir," answered a voice in the forest.

The master bridge builder shook his head and looked forlornly at Rollo. "You were brave . . . I was weak and cowardly."

"No, sir, I don't agree," answered Rollo. "Stygius Rex's magic is a powerful thing."

"But I told them everything they needed to know, who was useful, who wasn't." The old troll's voice quivered, and he covered his eyes with shame. "I was helpless to resist their questions. While you . . . *you* flew over that river as if you had wings. Just like this tiny being."

"Yes, but you broke free. Here you are!"

Krunkle nodded. "Thanks to the fact that you, Stygius Rex, and General Drool went off somewhere. As soon as you left for your adventure, I began to feel better. My wits came back to me, but I pretended to still be under his spell. By that time, they weren't paying much attention to me, so I was able to slip away."

The old troll shivered and held his crutch to his chest. "But the ghouls came after me. I could only get away from them by jumping off a cliff, and they left me for dead. Thankfully, our friends saw it from a distance and brought me here." He looked gratefully at the trolls gathered around him, and they smiled back with respect.

"More and more people come here every night," said Crawfleece, scanning the crowd. "I see about five new faces this morning. But there's little food, and ogres are all over the place."

Clipper whispered to Rollo, "I gather these ogres are not good?"

"They're just his servants, like us," answered Rollo. "Our real problem is with Stygius Rex. Does anybody know . . . did he ever come back from the Great Chasm?"

Krunkle shook his head and looked at the others, who answered with shrugs.

"Do you think it's safe for us to go home?" asked a child.

"No," answered Rollo sharply. "We saw ghouls on horseback last night, and they're still grabbing trolls for the work camp."

"The ogres are getting restless too," said Krunkle. "They didn't like being upstaged by a bunch of trolls in that flying business. I think they want to go home too."

"I think the biggest problem is food," chirped Clipper.

Everyone stopped to look at the diminutive fairy, and

she shrugged. "If you had enough food, you wouldn't need them at all. Wherever you lived would be fine."

"Spoken like a true troll!" thundered Krunkle. "Even though you're too small to be one. I agree with Clipper! Where can we find food, whether it belongs to us or not?"

"The ogre camp," said Rollo, "but I don't suggest we go there."

Crawfleece snapped her fingers and got a wide grin. "I know! In the Hole! We've seen at least a big snapper and a big sucker in there. We'll be poaching from Stygius Rex if we net them and eat them, but I say, 'Why not?'"

There were shouts of agreement, and the trolls began to jump up and down with excitement.

Clipper looked up at Rollo. "Do snapper and sucker taste good?"

The big troll gulped. "Only if you taste them before they taste you."

"Rollo, you have to lead them," said Krunkle suddenly. "Our little rebellion needs a leader, and that's you. If we could reach all the trolls in the work camp, we would have a trained army. They all cheered for you . . . they would follow you."

"Follow me into *what?*" asked Rollo. "A pitched battle with a crazy wizard who hurls fireballs? A war with ogres who have trained for years instead of days? I'm in this with you, but I don't know how far we can go. I'm just trying to save Clipper."

"Forget about me," said the little fairy. "Save Bonespittle."

"That's a great idea," replied Crawfleece, "but first we *eat*. To the Hole!" With a wave of her hand, she led the rag-tag band of trolls into the woods.

Rollo picked up Clipper and put her into his backpack, then he helped Master Krunkle to his feet. They hung back, letting the others charge ahead.

"You're making a joke, right?" he asked the old troll. "Just a week ago, I was a terrible apprentice, and now you want to put me in charge of all these trolls?"

Master Krunkle smiled. "I finally figured out what you were good at."

By the time they neared the Hole, Rollo, Clipper, and Krunkle were far behind the others, although they could hear the other voices floating through the sleepy grove. They weren't being as careful as they should be, thought Rollo worriedly. As in the Bonny Woods, there were no birdcalls, and the forest was eerily quiet.

The three of them had fallen into a watchful silence as they approached their destination. With every fiber of his hairy being, Rollo wanted to run and hide, but he didn't want to cause a false alarm. Clipper was asleep, snoring daintily, so she was no help. Krunkle did his best to shuffle along with his cane, but the old troll was near exhaustion.

You're going crazy, Rollo told himself. *There's nobody out there but mosquitoes as big as your thumb.*

The wind shifted, and the new breeze brought a strange smell—the stench of rancid meat. When Rollo got another sniff, he realized it wasn't so strange. He knew that smell!

From the black thickets came the sound of a sneeze.

"Master Krunkle," whispered Rollo, "take my pack and Clipper." He struggled to get out of the knapsack even as he quickened his step.

"Why?" asked the old troll, struggling to keep up.

"So that *you* can get on my back," answered Rollo urgently. "We've got to run."

His instincts told him to get away from the Hole, but he had to warn the others that they weren't alone. Rollo hoped he was wrong and that he smelled a dead tree rat, but that scent was too fresh in his mind.

He had spent days smelling it.

"What . . . where are we?" muttered Clipper, waking up when she was transferred to Krunkle.

Branches snapped behind them, and Rollo backed up against the old troll. "Hang on!"

He bent down, grabbed Krunkle's legs, and hoisted him onto his broad back. With a groan, Rollo took off running—just as a net flashed out of the dark branches. It dropped behind the young troll, making him run all the faster.

"Ogres! Ghouls!" he howled as he sprinted toward the

other trolls at the Hole. Screams and shouts erupted from the path ahead, and Rollo could see beastly figures moving in the shadows. Loud grunts, breaking branches, and crashing footsteps sounded all around, and Rollo knew they had been ambushed. Ogres were everywhere!

As Rollo staggered into the clearing, he could see more signs of a trap well sprung. Ogres charged out of the trees, tackling trolls, shooting nets, and threatening them with weapons. Rollo dashed forward and nearly ran headlong into the deep bog that was the Hole. His toes skidded to a stop just on the lip of the deadly pit, and a bit of dirt tumbled in.

"Rollo!"

The young troll whirled around to see Crawfleece on the ground with a fat ogre sitting on top of her. He was trying to tie her hands, but she kept fighting. The rest of the trolls were being captured and rounded up. With Krunkle and Clipper on his back, Rollo couldn't do much to help anyone. There was no escape with the Hole at his back.

"Get down, Master," he said, quickly lowering Krunkle. As the old troll sank to the soil, Clipper leaped from the bag onto Rollo's shoulder.

"Step away from the water," slurred a voice.

With a shudder, the young troll turned to see the gaunt, decomposed face of General Drool. His once-dapper clothes were dirty and torn, and his face was blackened by fireballs and lava. He looked like a pan full of burned snails, but the fires of evil burned brightly in his sunken eyes.

"Hand me the fairy," said the ghoul, reaching out with a skeletal hand.

Rollo realized that Drool feared he would throw Clipper into the brackish water of the Hole, or perhaps jump in himself. Several ogres pointed crossbows at him, loaded with nets, but they didn't seem to want to fire.

Sunlight twinkled through the sparse branches, and Rollo could see everyone clearly. Among the ogres, he spotted Captain Chomp and Lieutenant Weevil, who glared at him with a mixture of anger and awe. Everyone was standing still, staring at him. Then Rollo remembered he had a fairy perched on his shoulder, and that the ogres had never seen one of these radiant creatures before.

Clipper held her pose with dignity, but he could feel her shivering against his fur.

"Yes, Captain Chomp, this is a fairy," he told the brawny ogre. "For centuries, you big, bad ogres have gone to bed frightened to death of this teeny creature. General Drool's not afraid—he wants to enslave them, wipe them out. Do you want to build a massive bridge just to conquer this tiny race?"

General Drool sneezed loudly, blowing half his rotting brain onto Rollo's feet. He sniffed with a loud gurgling sound. "You're right, Troll. I'm weary of her and of you! You think you're smart, but I found you as soon as I got out of the Chasm. What I saw down there . . . never mind! I was led to you by the knife—*my* knife."

With surprise, Rollo gripped the black serpent knife he had forgotten was still stuck in his belt. He pulled it out to throw it away. That was the wrong thing to do, because General Drool promptly drew his sword as if he'd been challenged. Most of the ogres brandished their weapons and tensed for action. Rollo decided to hold on to the dagger.

"Like I said," slurred the ghoul, "I weary of *both* of you. The master isn't here to save you . . . no one is. We'll tell him you were killed while trying to escape."

After whirling the sword over his head, the gangly ghoul swung the blade at Rollo's stomach.

CHAPTER 19
ALLIES

As Rollo watched General Drool's sword, he remembered how to parry. When the general lunged, Rollo caught his sword with the crossguard of his dagger. The ghoul and the troll locked blades at the handles, and Rollo used his weight and muscle to push General Drool away from the edge of the Hole.

Once he was clear of the water, Rollo leaped back and looked for a way to escape. But every space in the bushes and trees was guarded by an ogre. The ghoul leveled his sword and was about to skewer Rollo when he suddenly spewed a tremendous sneeze. Clipper chuckled in Rollo's ear.

The troll used the seconds they gained to look around. He saw a thick vine hanging overhead, and he slashed it with his knife. Gripping the vine just like he did one innocent day not long ago, Rollo ran back and leaped into the air. That gave him a good backswing, and he went whooshing toward the Hole at high speed.

Just as General Drool recovered from his sneezing fit, Rollo plowed into him. The ghoul nearly dropped into the Hole, but at the last second he grabbed Rollo by the waist. With Clipper on top of the vine, Rollo in the middle, and General Drool hanging on, they went soaring over the murky water.

Rollo knew what was coming, and he tried to lift his legs. General Drool sputtered in anger, but he couldn't keep his legs from slicing through the muck. As he did, a huge tentacle whipped from the depths and lashed around Drool's throat. In the next instant, tremendous jaws rose from the water and clamped upon his waist.

The ghoul's strong arms gripped Rollo tightly and tried to drag him down into the mire. Instantly, the troll jammed his knife into Drool's hand and pried loose his grip. With a surprised gurgle, General Drool let go and plunged into the swirling depths.

Rollo's momentum was stopped, and he and Clipper hung over the Hole. Slashing jaws and lashing tentacles were only inches away, so Rollo stuck the knife in his belt and began to climb. General Drool was not so lucky, because the monsters pulled him down and tore him into bite-size bits. There wasn't a shred of him left in the teeming water, and the snapper and sucker fought over the last morsels.

They must be really hungry to eat that, thought Rollo with a shiver. He glanced around and saw ogres and trolls gaping in amazement at him. They were stunned speechless. They had obeyed General Drool for every day of their lives, and now the leader of the ghouls was really gone. No way were his body parts were going to get back together after that feast.

"That impressed them," Clipper whispered in his ear. "Now might be a good time to fly,"

"Maybe you're right," said the troll. "Hang on."

The fairy gripped the knot of hair on top of his head while Rollo concentrated on the wonderful sensation of flying. He was breathing hard from their narrow escape, but solid ground wasn't far away.

Rollo saw himself soaring over the Great Chasm like a bird—a clumsy bird but a good flyer nevertheless. When Rollo felt that familiar lightness in his stomach, he knew he was about to take off.

Trusting his instincts, he let go of the vine and lifted into the air. The onlookers gasped and made "ooh" and "aah" sounds, but it was a short flight. Rollo had barely gotten started when he landed on the far bank, near a mass of ogres.

"You killed General Drool!" rasped Captain Chomp in awe.

"I can't believe you did that," added Lieutenant Weevil. She seemed to be suppressing a smile.

"Then you *flew* in the air!" shouted Crawfleece in amazement.

"We told you he could," answered Clipper. "And it wasn't his fault that he had to fight your General Drool. You shouldn't hold it against him."

The ogres peered curiously at the boisterous fairy. "*This* is what they're like on the other side of the chasm?" asked Weevil.

Rollo nodded. "That's right. Clipper has a little magic, but the worst she can do is make you sneeze. Good thing that Drool was under her spell." He smiled at his tiny friend.

Master Krunkle staggered toward them. "Let us all go, Captain Chomp. You don't have to obey Stygius Rex anymore."

"Not obey Stygius Rex?" asked Chomp in a dazed voice. "Whom will we serve?"

"Serve yourselves," answered Rollo. "Be your own masters. That's what we trolls are going to do." The captured trolls shouted in agreement, and some of them jerked away from their captors.

Captain Chomp lifted his crossbow and aimed it at Rollo. "Are you planning to rebel?"

"I already have," answered Rollo truthfully. "I never planned to, but I did, anyway. We can't let Stygius Rex run our lives anymore—he's crazy with power and greed. Do you want to spend the rest of your life—maybe give up your life—to build a stupid bridge?"

The squat ogre grumbled and shook his head. "We ogres never thought we could fly, and Stygius Rex just made us look bad. Then we spent a week cooking and cleaning for all you trolls! On top of that, we had to teach you how to *fight*. Your little rebellion shows how stupid *that* was. But what if Stygius Rex isn't dead?"

Rollo leaned forward excitedly. "Without the ogres, he's nothing. We know the ghouls will obey him, but there aren't that many of them. We can beat them in a fight."

"We're pledged to Stygius Rex!" said Captain Chomp with alarm. "We can't fight with you . . . against him."

"I don't want you to fight at all!" pleaded Rollo. "I want you to do *nothing*. Take a day off. We know we'll have to fight the ghouls, and we're ready for that. We'll fight Stygius Rex, too, if he comes back, but we don't want to fight the ogres. I figure we will if we have to."

Rollo gave his old nemesis a smile. "Captain, you were the one who told us there are enough trolls to do whatever we want, if we just band together. I think we're ready to do it."

"Overthrow the master?" Chomp asked doubtfully, as if it couldn't be done.

Rollo countered, "For two hundred years we've been ruled by a stingy old sorcerer. Enough is enough! I'm not asking you to rebel against anyone, Captain Chomp, I'm just asking you to take a night or two off. Go fishing."

Chomp looked confused over what to do, and Weevil cleared her throat. "Captain," she whispered, "we could send the whole ogre army out to search for our missing leaders. Those are our orders from Runt—to search until we find them. But nobody knows that we found Rollo or General Drool, except this squad. And we're all loyal to you."

"That's good to know," muttered the big ogre with a snort. "Rollo, the ogres will be gone from camp tonight and tomorrow night. We'll return day after tomorrow. Do your business and do it well, or prepare to face us."

"Yes, Captain," said Rollo, springing to attention. "Thank you, sir. We'll do the job."

"We'll leave you some food, too." He glanced past Rollo's shoulder and shook his head in awe. "And guard that little fairy. I believe you can't succeed without her."

"I know it," answered Rollo.

Chomp waved to his squad and bellowed, "Release the prisoners, and leave your rations with them! We'll get the horses and return to camp."

After the food was distributed and gratefully accepted, Chomp organized his troops and marched them off into the forest. Hungrily, the trolls ate the gopher jerky and dried leech pie. Clipper took a bite of the ogre rations and decided that she would rather look for berries in the thickets.

"Hey, look!" said Crawfleece, pointing into the Hole. Her voice was so sharp that everyone stopped their ravenous eating to gaze into the pit. Rollo could hardly believe his eyes.

The scaly snapper floated on the water like a log, and the tentacled sucker looked like a giant pink lily pad. Neither one of them moved as they bobbed up and down in the soupy mire.

"The monsters died from eating General Drool," said Krunkle. "Can't have been good for them."

"We could fish them out and cook them," suggested a child.

"No thanks," answered Crawfleece, putting down her food. "I kind of lost my appetite. From now on, it just won't be as much fun skimming the Hole."

"Look," said Rollo, "there's plenty of food in the ogre camp, and in a few hours, they'll be gone. Let's get everyone in the town to come with us. They'll follow us anywhere as long as we promise them food."

"They'll follow *you* anyway," said Krunkle, "after we tell them you killed General Drool."

"But I . . . it wasn't me . . . it was those—" He pointed to the dead monsters floating in the bog, but they didn't seem very menacing.

"We'll tell them," insisted Krunkle, pointing to the three dozen trolls gathered around. All of them nodded solemnly, and even Crawfleece beamed with pride. "We'll tell them that the trolls finally have a leader who *is* a troll."

As they cheered him, Rollo nodded sheepishly. They couldn't be talking about *him,* could they? But they were. *I need a plan,* thought Rollo. *A good plan.*

CHAPTER 20

RECKONING

"HEY! WATCH IT! LOOK OUT!" SHOUTED RUNT, HOPPING around like a gnome whose pants were on fire. They were stepping on one another's feet—he and ten ghouls—all of whom were trying to throw ropes over Old Belch. The giant toad was upset, and with one big jump he would be out of his corral. Nobody knew what had gotten into him.

What a day for all the ogres to be gone! thought Runt with chagrin. *And where is the only one who can handle this beast—Stygius Rex?*

He thought maybe the trolls would help, but they were all hiding in their barracks. It was a bright, sunny day, and he should be underground sleeping. Instead, the gnome was trying to wrangle a huge amphibian ten times his size.

"Braaappp!" belched the beast, blowing Runt's hat off

with the force of his putrid breath. The little gnome staggered, but he stayed on his feet.

"You behave yourself, you stupid bag of warts!" shouted the angry gnome. "Or we're going to give the fresh maggots to the trolls—and not you!"

Without warning, the giant toad took a short hop over his corral, flattening three ghouls. The others shrieked and ran in terror, throwing their ropes into the air. All Runt could do was scurry out of the way before the toad decided to jump toward him.

The ground shuddered when Old Belch leaped again, and two tents were flattened. Nobody tried to stop the toad this time as he hopped toward the Rawchill River. Runt ran after him just to see what the monster would do. With a mighty leap, the great toad vaulted over the river and disappeared into the mist.

Runt spent the next few minutes stomping the ground and cursing himself. How was he going to tell Stygius Rex that they had lost Old Belch? Of course, there was a chance that Stygius Rex wasn't coming back. And neither was General Drool. If that happened, there wouldn't be any need to explain, because Runt would be in charge of this rowdy bunch.

When I'm in charge, it will be back to sleeping days and staying underground, Runt decided.

After making that decision, the gnome felt better. He leaped to his feet and motioned to the collection of ghouls who had followed him to the river. "All of you ghouls, get back to your posts! Don't let any more trolls escape, either, or you'll have to answer to *me!*"

The ghouls looked mildly confused by these orders, and they bumped into one another as they scattered. Runt could only sit on the misty banks of the Rawchill River and think about this strange turn of events. He was in charge of Bonespittle, and it might not be temporary.

Runt had a hard time imagining himself in charge. Then again, he had a hard time imagining *anyone* else in charge but Stygius Rex. A sorcerer, or a bunch of sorcerers, had been in charge of Bonespittle ever since anyone could remember. The wizened little gnome was frightened by his own thoughts, but he had to consider them.

Who will run Bonespittle if Stygius Rex doesn't return?

Even if General Drool came back, that still left a power vacuum. It was hard to imagine the whole country being run by a dead body. The ogres might try to take over, and they had the muscle and weapons to do it. Maybe it was a good thing they were all gone for a while.

Runt knew he had to plan for every likelihood. He didn't have to seize power, because he was already in power. The question was, how to hold on to his status?

I'll just have to earn their trust by making wise decisions. Runt frowned, because that sounded hard. Better yet, he would find someone who would frighten the subjects into obedience for him! He would stay in the background and call the shots. Yes, that was a workable plan!

Now who would fit the bill? The squat gnome sat on the bank of the river, mulling over his choices. The ghouls were scary, but none of them had the gruesome charisma of General Drool. The most likely candidate would be Captain Chomp; at least he could keep the ogres in line.

But why would Chomp need me? wondered Runt, arguing against himself. Feeling confused, the gnome did what he always did: He crawled into his hole and went to sleep.

"Master Runt! Master Runt!" said a gruff voice, shaking him out of his dreamless sleep.

"Huh? What is it? I thought I left word not to be disturbed!" The gnome opened his eyes cautiously, expecting to see the dreaded sunlight. But the only light in the underground chamber was the lantern in the ghoul's hand.

"Trolls!" said the ghoul, who was named Spectre. "Thousands of them are at the gate!"

Runt sat up and rubbed his eyes. "What do they want?"

"They want to join the work crew," answered the ghoul. "They say there's no food in the swamp anymore—and no work—so the only way to *eat* is to build the bridge."

The little gnome grabbed a pointed green hat and leaped out of his sleeping pit. "We spend a week stealing them from their muddy hovels, and now they show up *wanting* to work? Trolls can be so fickle!"

"Plus, there's no bridge, is there?" asked Spectre.

"Do you see one?" Runt crawled past the ghoul and

climbed up the burrow toward the upper hatch. He didn't see any light when he emerged into the cool, misty air, and that was fine with him.

"Ah, nighttime!" said the gnome with relief. "All that sunlight is terrible for my complexion." He rubbed his most prized, hairiest wart to make sure it was okay.

Spectre, the ghoul, followed him out. "They're at the gate of the stockade, sir."

"I'm not going to face them alone—get all the ghouls to come with me," ordered Runt.

"But, Master, they are guarding *our* trolls, who are cooking their own food."

"The trolls won't go anywhere as long as we have food—get me a guard of ghouls!"

"Yes, Master." Spectre bowed like a cadaverous undertaker, then shuffled off.

While he was gone, Runt surveyed the dark camp, which seemed empty without the ogres. He could see rows of tents and distant torches along the wall of the stockade. It wasn't a very big wall; it was made hastily of wooden poles, and it wouldn't survive an assault by thousands of trolls.

He couldn't believe that he had let Captain Chomp take every ogre into the field. Their trolls had been sitting around for days, doing nothing but eating. No one considered them a threat. Now a bunch of disgruntled trolls from outside showed up, causing trouble. All because they wanted food!

What happened to the art of digging for grubs?

Food, thought Runt with a twitch of his ample nose. *That's was all they really wanted.* Runt grinned a snaggletoothed smile, because he had a plan to get rid of these hungry trolls. *Feed them!* In another couple of days, he would send all the trolls home, and everything would be back to normal.

Except that I'll be in charge, decided Runt.

He heard shuffling sounds, and he turned to see Spectre, leading about twenty ghouls toward him. When seen in a mob, the ghouls were very eerie and impressive. They should be enough to ward off a few disgruntled trolls.

"Come on!" ordered Runt, leading the way toward the main gate.

When the gnome and his entourage approached the iron bars, his mood turned cheerful. It was mostly a crowd of pathetic children and elders, looking ragged and hungry. True, their numbers stretched into the shadowy distance, but these starved trolls were not any sort of threat.

"Listen," said Runt magnanimously, "by order of Stygius Rex, who is *resting* at the moment, I have been instructed to feed all of you!"

That brought tremendous cheers from the crowd of trolls, and Runt already felt like a beloved leader. "Open the gate!"

The ghoul who manned the pulley chains looked askance at Runt, but he still lifted the gate. As soon as the metal bars rose high enough, trolls poured into the stockade. It was like a stampede, forcing Runt to scurry back to the protection of the ghouls.

The trolls swarmed over his new position as well, and Runt was surprised to see they were *big* trolls. Where were the hungry children?

Before the gnome could blink, the trolls flung nets over the sluggish ghouls. The undead soldiers stumbled and collapsed before they could even draw their swords. Behind this first wave came a second wave of trolls with rocks and wooden planks in their hands. It wasn't long before they were breaking up the ghouls into very small pieces.

Runt was glad to be short, because he was able to run through legs and under the nets, avoiding the mayhem. He scooted across the dirt, trying to reach his burrow, but a strange flying creature suddenly darted in front of him. It was as big as a troll. It *was* a troll!

"Halt right there!" cried a tiny voice, and Runt realized there was a second creature perched on the shoulder of the first. This being was even smaller than a gnome—lithe, pale, and shimmering—unlike anything he had ever seen in Bonespittle.

That scared Runt to death, and he turned to flee when a net dropped over him. The gnome rolled along the ground and was grabbed by the flying troll as he landed. Of course, it was Rollo, he realized. *How many other flying trolls do I know?*

Rollo held up the net to inspect the struggling gnome.

Also inspecting him was the strange, shimmering sprite perched on his shoulder. Surely it was some kind of foul demon from the Bonny Woods!

"How dare you! You ungrateful troll!" shouted the gnome, trying to maintain an air of authority. "After everything we've done for you, Rollo, this is how you repay us? Call off your brutes. Stop smashing up my ghouls!"

"What is this creature?" asked the fey thing on the troll's shoulder.

"It's a gnome," answered Rollo. "We don't see them too often, but this one we've seen too much."

"Do you have to cut it up, like they're doing with the ghouls?" Sawing and hacking noises filled the night air.

"I don't think so," answered Rollo thoughtfully. "But maybe."

"Help! Help!" shouted Runt, twisting and squirming.

"But probably not," Rollo added. "We have to cut up the ghouls to keep their bodies from rejoining, but we're really doing them a favor."

"Since they're already dead," said Clipper, wincing with distaste. "What will you do with this gnome?"

Rollo drew a black knife that looked familiar and held it where Runt could see it. "Stygius Rex isn't really here, is he?"

The gnome tightened his lips, and Rollo moved the blade closer. "If you think they'll save you, they won't. Look at this serpent knife. It once belonged to General Drool, and he came after me because of it. But now the ghoul is dead. In fact, *all* the ghouls are dead, the ogres are gone, and the only sorcerer is missing. So I suggest you cooperate with us."

Rollo pointed to the delicate being on his shoulder. "And this is a fairy. Her name is Clipper. You see, I've been to the other side of the Great Chasm and have returned, unlike Stygius Rex. She's not as dangerous as we were told, but the part about her magic is true. Clipper, would you care to turn this gnome into a dung heap?"

The fairy considered the proposal for a moment. "What kind of dung would you like? I can turn him into ferret dung, wombat dung, or camel dung."

"No, no! We can talk!" shouted the gnome, pretending to be afraid. In reality, his mind was working feverishly. "Let me look at that knife."

Rollo held it up again, and the gnome nodded his head. "Yes, I recognize Drool's knife. Do you know its power?"

"What power?" asked Rollo.

Runt squirmed some more. "Let me go, and I'll tell you."

"You seem to forget exactly who's in charge here," said Rollo. "I don't want to hurt you, because you were nice to me . . . I think. But we trolls are tired of being pushed around. Tell me the truth, have you heard from Stygius Rex?"

"No," answered Runt truthfully. As he stared at the hulking troll, he made up his mind. Here was the big, menacing presence he needed to be the muscle in his new regime. And Rollo had thousands of trolls who would follow him. Replace the ogres with trolls—it sounded okay to him.

"I've been wondering what to do," said Runt, "if the master and the general are truly gone. We're still feeding the workers, and they're happy. I was about to feed all of *you* when you turned on me like vipers. Well done, Rollo! You have a great future in politics. I've got no problem working with you trolls."

"Rollo!" yelled a voice, followed by a chorus of voices shouting the troll's name. The flying troll was suddenly surrounded by new arrivals from the camp; some of them still had food in their hands.

They slapped him on the back and all talked at once. They included his tent mates and his father, Nulneck. It was a disgustingly happy reunion.

"Son, I can't believe you're here!" bellowed Rollo's father, gripping him in a tearful hug. "I've heard so many incredible things about you. Those stories can't all be true!"

After they met the amazing fairy, it was clear that the stories *must* be true. In all this excitement, Runt hoped he would get misplaced, but Rollo clutched the netted gnome tightly to his chest.

The young troll told a short version of his adventures, and even Runt couldn't help but be impressed by his pluck. Rollo ended by saying, "We've got to pack up and take our food home. Quick, before the ogres get back."

"Wait a minute!" said a stumpy troll who had just arrived. "It's me—your old friend Filbum! Why should we leave, Rollo? We never had it better than we do here." There were murmured shouts of agreement, and Runt was jostled some more.

"Because your families are at home starving!" answered Rollo. "Because the food won't last, because we're not building the bridge, because it's all over! The reign of Stygius Rex is over."

Suddenly the ground shuddered, as if something huge had dropped upon the earth. "Braaapp!" The air exploded with the loudest eruption of reeking breath that any troll had ever survived. The raunchy wind knocked Rollo back on his heels.

"I wouldn't be too sure it's over," said Runt with a chuckle.

CHAPTER 21

FOR THE BAD OF BONESPITTLE

R OLLO WHIRLED AROUND TO SEE THE GIANT TOAD VAULT over the wall and land in the clearing. Trolls scattered in all directions from Old Belch, and their fear mounted when they got a good look at the monster. Sitting astride the behemoth was the black-shrouded figure of Stygius Rex, holding a lantern in his hands.

The squirming gnome in his arms didn't seem so important, and Rollo dropped Runt to the ground. The gnome scampered away as Clipper gripped Rollo's fur tightly. The young troll looked for his mates and family, but Filbum, Krunkle, Crawfleece, and Nulneck were nowhere to be found. The trolls had melted into the darkness with a skill born from centuries of practice.

The only one who could not run away was Rollo. That was because he had a fairy perched on his shoulder, and Clipper's presence made him brave.

Stygius Rex was seething with anger. "Oh, stupid little troll, you have been very bad indeed! You killed my ghouls, which took me much time and trouble to raise. I pity you when General Drool returns—"

"Him, too!" shouted Rollo in a squeaky voice. "I killed him, too."

"I truly misjudged you," hissed the sorcerer, lowering his hooded gaze at Rollo. "I won't do that again. At least you have kept my fairy safe, but it doesn't matter. I have enough information to invade the Bonny Woods—without the bridge or the fairy. I don't need either of you."

That was when Rollo realized that the lantern in the mage's hand wasn't really a lantern—it was a fireball!

He dove to the ground just as the fireball streaked along the ground and seared his backside. It swerved into an empty barracks and blew it up with a shimmering plume of sparks. Stygius Rex was a better shot on open terrain, and Rollo realized he and Clipper were in plain sight.

Mustering all his willpower, the troll envisioned himself lifting high into the air. He could feel Clipper on his shoulder, digging her fingernails into his skin. Reaching toward the sky, Rollo shot upward as another fireball whooshed under his feet. It demolished a row of tents, setting all of them ablaze.

As he rose, Rollo glanced down and saw bedlam below him, with trolls fleeing in droves from the fire. Some of them even rushed to the riverbank, hoping the frigid water would protect them. Staying on the giant toad, Stygius Rex scanned the sky for his enemy.

Hovering above the smoke from all the fires, Rollo was a poor target. He knew he could escape by flying, but that would leave the trolls at the mercy of Stygius Rex again. If the ogres returned and found the sorcerer alive, they would go back to serving him. Then the rebellion of the trolls would be over.

At the mage's command, Old Belch took a jump and landed right under Rollo. At once, a fireball shot high into the air and zoomed past the troll, showering him with flaming sparks. Patting out his burning fur, Rollo tried to fly higher, but Stygius had the troll in his sights. Another fireball streaked past him, scorching the air and making it hard to breathe.

Panting, Rollo turned to Clipper and rasped, "How do we fight him?"

"The toad!" she answered urgently. "Get me close enough, and I'll make him jump."

Rollo dropped lower through the smoke, keeping his eyes on Old Belch. The great toad looked glassy-eyed and immobile, like some kind of speckled boulder. *He's under a spell,* thought Rollo. *The sorcerer is casting a lot of spells, so he must be growing weaker. That's why he can't move around.*

"Closer!" urged Clipper, whispering in his ear. Rollo zoomed toward the toad and his rider, not knowing what the fairy was going to do.

Stygius Rex raised his hand and launched another fireball, which came speeding toward Rollo. The troll tilted sideways, and the flame roared past him, sizzling and popping with sparks.

"Keep going!" cried Clipper in his ear. "Fly over the toad!"

Rollo sped toward his huge target, gravity making him go faster. As he whooshed over Old Belch, he felt something spring off his shoulder. Rollo gasped when he saw Clipper go spinning down through the smoke, steering herself with her good wing. He wanted to dive after her, but Stygius caught sight of him and raised his arm.

A fireball careened past Rollo, causing him to spin into several wild loops. Using all his concentration, the troll just managed to stay in the air. He was trying to turn around and come back for Clipper when the night was ruptured by a grunting shriek.

Rollo turned to see Old Belch take off like a shot, with the sorcerer barely clinging to his back. The toad jumped so high that he flew past Rollo, just missing him by a few feet. The troll thought he saw Clipper clinging to a strap on the toad's saddle. At least it looked like something wispy and white.

Old Belch soared over Rollo's head and dropped toward the rushing river, with the stunned sorcerer clinging to his back. Rollo had a hard time keeping up, and it was clear that Old Belch was not going to stop on the bank. The giant toad vaulted into the water with a huge splash, hit the bottom, and lunged out again.

That was when Stygius Rex flew off his mount, rising swiftly into the air. Rollo closed on the wizard, and he could see Clipper latched to Stygius's face, kicking him with her tiny feet. Both of them were dripping wet and shivering. The sorcerer's head bobbed up and down, because he was sneezing furiously.

Picking up speed, Rollo slammed into the wizard. They whirled in the air like leaves caught in a storm, then they plummeted toward the frenzied rapids. Rollo tried to grasp Clipper, but the enraged sorcerer plucked the fairy from his face and hurled her into the darkness.

"You must die!" he screamed, wrapping his bony fingers around Rollo's neck.

They crashed into the frigid waves, and Rollo's breath was sucked out of him by the cold. Nevertheless, he managed to clutch Stygius Rex and hold him in his strong grip. They grappled underwater, and Rollo could feel the aged creature growing weak. Then both of them were slammed into a submerged rock, and the current tore the mage out of his grasp.

With a crushing pain on his left side, Rollo could barely move his arms to hold on to the rock. Tearfully, he searched the churning water for Clipper, but he couldn't see her. Finally the current pulled him off the rock, and Rollo went tumbling through the rapids. Shaken by pain and cold, he was unable to draw a breath—the young troll was certain he was going to drown.

Just as the current was about to drag him under for good, strong arms grabbed him. As Rollo was yanked to the surface, he sputtered and waved his arms. His saviors had to fight both him and the current to drape him over a rope. With a start, Rollo realized it was the same lifeline they had strung across the river many days ago.

Through his tears and the stinging water, Rollo could see the beaming face of his sister and the terror-stricken face of his friend, Filbum. All three of them were drenched and half-drowned, but they were alive and clinging weakly to the lifeline.

"Are you all right?" asked Crawfleece with concern. She had to shout over the rushing water.

"No!" wailed Rollo. "Where's Clipper? Have you seen her?"

"Is she out here?" asked Crawfleece in amazement. She shook her bushy head, and a spray of water went flying. "We were lucky to spot *you* . . . and lucky that Filbum thought about the lifeline."

"I must be crazy!" shouted Filbum with a terrified laugh. "I wouldn't risk my life for anybody but you!"

"We've got to find Clipper!" wailed the young troll, struggling to get back into the water.

"No! No!" shouted Crawfleece. "We didn't save you to

see you drown again! I don't know where the fairy is, but *you* have to live! There are about ten thousand trolls waiting on the bank for you." She began to pull him along the rope.

"Stygius Rex?" asked Rollo, gazing uncertainly at the churning rapids.

"I think I saw him wash by," answered Filbum, his teeth chattering. "Come on, we've got to get out of here!"

Rollo knew they were right, and no amount of grief or guilt would bring Clipper back. Stifling his tears and the pain, he pulled himself along the rope. "Clipper!" he called one last time. "Clipper!"

"We'll walk along the river and keep looking for her," said Crawfleece. "But let's get out of here, like we planned."

"You beat them, Rollo!" cried Filbum, slapping his painful shoulder. "You beat them all!"

Rollo winced and grunted weakly. It didn't feel like he had won—it felt as if he had lost.

CHAPTER 22
LOST AND FOUND

ROLLO SAT ON THE TOP OF THE MOUND WHERE HIS FAMILY lived. His mouth hanging open, he surveyed lines of trolls, branching out in all directions on all the bridges. It was morning, and he could finally see how many were waiting. They stood patiently, gazing at the young troll and smiling.

They just wanted to meet the troll who had vanquished both Stygius Rex and General Drool. They wanted to shake his hand and touch his fur. Rollo had led them in a revolt against the dreaded ghouls, whose remains were scattered all over Bonespittle. Plus, he had released everyone in the work camp and brought back tons of food. He had even made peace with the ogres.

There was no end to what the young troll could do, or so it seemed. He was their hero, their new leader. But the one thing Rollo really wanted to do he couldn't do: He couldn't bring Clipper back to life.

His assistants—Crawfleece, Krunkle, and Filbum—had to usher him through his well-wishers. With so many to see, he could only spend a few seconds with each one. Rollo was getting weary of the endless greetings, saying the same things over and over—but he didn't want to disappoint anyone. Trolls had waited a long time to be free.

They had never had a ruler who was one of them, some-one they could walk up to and say hello. Rollo would try to be what they wanted—what they needed—but he was afraid he would disappoint them.

"Thank you," he said again for the three hundredth time. "Yes, I saw you fighting the ghouls, and we really needed your help. Keep working for the good of Troll Town."

"This way," said Filbum, ushering the happy subject away.

Rollo's eyes glazed over as he surveyed the hundreds still waiting to see him. Suddenly a face leaped out of the crowd—a terrifically hideous face!

"Ludicra!" exclaimed Rollo, jumping to his feet. He pushed his way through the crowd in order to reach his beloved. When they met, he wanted to take her in his arms, but that would be undignified for the new ruler. He hadn't hugged any of the rest of his subjects. "Ludicra, where have you been?" he asked dumbly.

"Hiding. My father made us leave the village." She

looked down demurely and batted her scraggly eyebrows. "They say you're the new ruler of all trolls . . . and maybe all of Bonespittle. The Troll King."

Rollo rolled his eyes. "I don't know about being a 'king.' I'm just a troll who did something that had to be done."

"Anyway," said Ludicra sweetly, "I know I wasn't very nice to you before, but all of that has changed. My parents even like you now."

"Do they?" asked Rollo. Suddenly the feelings he had for Ludicra were beginning to fade.

"They think we ought to start making plans," said Ludicra. "You know, in case you need a queen."

"I'm not a ruler yet," said Rollo. In the distance, a commotion on the bridge caught his eye, and he could see someone trying to squeeze past the waiting trolls. As he looked more closely, he could tell that it was a party of ogres, and one of them was carrying something smaller.

"Let them pass!" called Rollo, waving his arms. "Let the ogres pass!"

As the crowd parted and the ogres moved closer, Rollo could see Captain Chomp in the lead. Behind him came Lieutenant Weevil, who was carrying the gnome, Runt, on her shoulders.

"What's going on here?" asked Chomp with a toothy grin. "Your coronation?"

"Not quite yet," muttered Rollo. "What brings you to Dismal Swamp, Captain?"

"This." The big ogre held up a small box about a foot long, and Rollo's heart sank down to his knees. He knew without being told what was in the box. Rollo pushed Ludicra out of the way in order to go meet them.

"You found Clipper?" he asked.

"Yes!" said Runt quickly. "*We* found her . . . the gnomes and ogres. I made them keep looking for her!"

"We were looking for Stygius Rex too," said Chomp with a scowl. "We never found a trace of him. As for the fairy . . . well, this is for you." He held out the small rectangular box.

With trembling hands and a trembling lip, Rollo took the container from the big ogre. The crowd of trolls hushed all around them; even those who hadn't seen the fairy had heard the stories about her.

Rollo felt warm fur near him, and he turned to see his family—Vulgalia, Nulneck, and Crawfleece—gathering near. Their gloomy faces showed how sad they were, both for Clipper and for Rollo. Vulgalia gave Rollo a hug, which brought a painful twinge to his banged-up shoulder.

He started to open the box, and Weevil reached out a hand to stop him. "Don't open it," she cautioned.

"Why? Clipper's in here, isn't she?"

"Yes," answered Weevil. "But that box is made of coffin wood, and it has properties that preserve a body."

"Why should we need to do that?" asked Rollo. "She's dead, isn't she?"

"Yes, but we found her in extremely cold water, so her

body hasn't gone bad." Weevil looked up at the gnome sitting on her shoulder. "Perhaps you should tell him."

"Yes, yes!" said Runt eagerly. "It was *my* idea, Rollo, to preserve her body. Do you still have the knife you got from General Drool?"

"Why, yes," answered Rollo with confusion. He touched the handle of the serpent blade in his belt. Although many times he had almost thrown the weapon away, each time he eventually had decided to keep it. The strange knife had saved his life when he was fighting General Drool, even though it had led the ghoul to him.

"I told you that knife was special," said Runt. "It's a tool that Stygius Rex uses to raise the dead and make ghouls. He used it to make General Drool, which is why the ghoul always knew where it was."

Rollo drew the serpentine blade and studied it. "Do you mean I could bring her back to life with this? *How?*"

The gnome shook his head. "That I don't know. None of us are sorcerers. I just thought you should know about it . . . and that there's a chance to save her. If you can find a master of magic."

"The other fairies," said Rollo, a glimmer of hope brightening his rubbery face. He turned to his parents and hugged them. His lips were trembling, and he could barely bring himself to speak. "Mother, Father—"

His sister jumped in. "You're going back across the Great Chasm, aren't you?"

Rollo nodded. When his mother burst into tears, he gave her an extra hug. "I'll make sure to come home . . . even if I have to fly all the way."

"What about these thousands of people?" asked Filbum. "What about crowning you *king?*"

"That will have to wait," answered Rollo, gripping the box to his chest and starting across the nearest bridge. "Father! You're in charge until I return. Make that . . . you and Runt are in charge. The gnome can read and write and organize—he'll be a great help to you."

"I won't let you down!" shouted Runt happily.

"Those elves and fairies are likely to kill you at first sight," warned Captain Chomp.

"I'll deal with them." Rollo stuck the knife back in his belt and made sure it was secure.

"What about our wedding?" screamed Ludicra, shaking her fists in the air.

Rollo could only wave at her as he hurried off, muscling his way onto another bridge. Even though he couldn't open the box to see Clipper, he knew she was in there. He could feel her presence.

Other trolls watched dumbfounded as their hero scurried past, leaving Troll Town. Most of them wondered if they would ever see Rollo again; the others wondered if they would ever see another flying troll. Rollo wondered whether he would ever see Stygius Rex again.

As usual, he felt guilty about his actions, but he had done

enough for his fellow trolls. It was up to them to take it from here. All of Bonespittle was better off without those two, Stygius Rex and General Drool. He had yet to hear of anyone who mourned them.

Still, he mourned for Clipper and the harm they had done to the Bonny Woods. Before this misadventure, the Great Chasm had separated strangers; now it separated enemies. *I have to close that rift,* thought Rollo.

As he scrambled up a muddy mound and down a shaky bridge, the troll hugged the box to his chest. "I promised you I would take you home," he whispered, "and I will."

ABOUT THE AUTHOR

JOHN VORNHOLT HAS HAD SEVERAL WRITING AND PERFORMING careers, ranging from being a stuntman in the movies to writing animated cartoons. After spending fifteen years as a freelance journalist, John turned to book publishing in 1989. Drawing upon the goodwill generated by an earlier nonfiction book he had written, John secured a contract to write *Masks,* number seven in the *Star Trek: The Next Generation*™ book series.

Masks was the first of the numbered *Next Generation* books to make the *New York Times* best-seller list and was reprinted three times in the first month. John has seen several of his *Star Trek*™ books make the *Times* best-seller list. Since then, he has written and sold more than fifty books for both adults and children.

Theatrical rights for his fantasy novel about Aesop, *The Fabulist,* have been sold to David Spencer and Stephen Witkin in New York. They're in the process of adapting it as a Broadway musical. John currently lives with his wife and two children in Tucson, Arizona. Please visit his Web site at: www.vornholt.net.

Visit *The Troll King* Web site: www.troll-king.com.

THE YORK TRILOGY
BY PHYLLIS REYNOLDS NAYLOR

Shadows on the Wall
0-689-84961-3 $4.99

Faces in the Water
0-689-84962-1 $4.99

Footprints at the Window
0-689-84963-X $4.99